# THE CAPTAIN'S BOMBSHELL

Adam Carter

Copyright 2019, © Adam Carter. All rights reserved. No content may be reproduced without permission of the author.

Cover Design by James, GoOnWrite.com

Visit: https://www.facebook.com/OperationWetFish for news, illustrations, previews and short stories.

For Paul

# The Captain's Bombshell

Also available by the same author:

Dinosaur World books:
- Excavating a Dinosaur World
- Dinosaur Fall-Girl
- Dinosaur Plague Doctor
- Ike Scarman & the Dinosaur Slavers of Ceres
- Dinosaur Prison World
- The Dinosaur That Wasn't
- Awfully Wedded Strife
- Tales of a Dinosaur Prison World
- Deities of a Dinosaur World
- Return to the Dinosaur Prison World
- Nikolina Finch & the Dinosaur Utopia
- Of Stags, Hens & Dinosaurs
- Dinosaur World Gladiator
- The Wounding Tooth
- Dinosaur World Massacre
- Dino-Racers
- Dinosaur World Unscripted
- Christmas on a Dinosaur World
- Utara the Savage

Sheriff Grizzly:
- Book 1: Sheriff Grizzly
- Book 2: The Horse Thief Honey
- Book 3: The Coyote Colt Kid
- Book 4: Joins the Circus
- Book 5: The Haunting of Athelstan Swift
- Book 6: The Santa Claws Showdown
- Book 7: The Kangaroo Claim Jumpers of Crumbling Gulch
- Book 8: Gets a Reality Check
- Book 9: Bets Against the Card Shark
- Book 10: The Hairy Walrus of Truespire Peak
- Book 11: The End
- Book 12: In the Afterlife

Knights of Torbalia gamebooks:
- The Return of the Stolen Jewel
- Into the Massacre
- March of the Demon Trees
- The Thief of Tarley Manor
- The Class War
- The Haunting of Past Wraiths
- The Hunt for the Adulterous Bard
- A Peacock in the Den of Foxes
- Attack of the Demon Trees
- The Slave Scandal of Torbalia

Miscellaneous gamebooks:
- Lost Treasures of a Dinosaur World (300 paragraphs)
- The Underworld Horror (300 paragraphs)
- Sheriff Grizzly: The Good, the Bad & the Grizzly
- Sheriff Grizzly: The Wild West Dungeon Adventure
- The Christmas Adventure of Sam and Klutz
- Operation WetFish: Vengeful Justice
- Operation WetFish: A Wealth of Sin
- Jupiter's Glory: Oppression of the Press
- Dinosaur World: The Forest of Fiends
- The Temple of Death: The Villain's Gamebook

Hero Cast trilogy:
- Book 1: The Villainous Heroes
- Book 2: The Heroic Villains
- Book 3: The Forge of Heroes

Jupiter's Glory:
- Book 1: The Dinosaur World
- Book 2: The Pirates and the Priests
- Book 3: The Obsidian Slavers
- Book 4: Just Passing Through
- Book 5: The Virus of Gangrene's Scurvy
- Book 6: Stranded on a Storm Moon
- Book 7: Eyes on the Prize

# Adam Carter

Detective books:
- Detective's Ex
- One-Way Ticket to Murder
- Who Slew Santa?
- The Curse of the Genie's Detective
- The Woman Who Cried Diamonds
- The Murder of Snowman Joe
- The Murder of Loyalty
- The Prostitute Butcher
- The Santa Worshippers
- Betty Stalks a Biker Cop

Dinosaur Frontier:
- Book 1: The Lightning Angel
- Book 2: Lightning Strikes Twice
- Book 3: The Law of Ceres
- Book 4: The Silk Caves of Ceres

Operation WetFish, Vampire Detective:
- Book 1: The Power of Life and Death
- Book 2: Chasing Innocence
- Book 3: The Hunt for Charles Baronaire
- Book 4: Christmas on the Kerb
- Book 5: A Necessary Evil
- Book 6: No Comment
- Book 7: Fear and Ecstasy
- Book 8: Call of the Siren
- Book 9: Happy Families
- Book 10: A Step in the Right Direction
- Book 11: What Money Can't Buy
- Book 12: 'Tis the Season
- Book 13: The Power Trip
- Book 14: Trust and Betrayal
- Book 15: A Gathering of Minds
- Book 16: The Pain of Life
- Book 17: The Happy Place
- Book 18: The Terrible Truth of Barry Stockwell
- Book 19: The Apex Predator
- Book 20: End of an Era
- Book 21: He Who Kills the Killers' Killers
- Book 22: Bad Day at the Office
- Book 23: Death of the Dream
- Book 24: Out for Blood
- Book 25: Reckoning
- Book 26: Pillow Talk
- Book 27: For the Greater Good
- Book 28: The Plot to Kill the King

Miscellaneous:
- Holding the Nuts
- One Week to Love: Speed Dating of the Gods
- The Trojan Ant
- Gauntlet of Daedalus
- The Faerie Contract
- Token Love
- Sleigh Ride Slaughter to Saturn
- Have Imagination, Will Travel
- A Mermaid's Odyssey

# THE CAPTAIN'S BOMBSHELL

# CHAPTER ONE

The sun was shining and the air was warm, but that was what life at the seaside was all about. I had lived by the sea my whole life and had never wanted to be anywhere else. When I was a little girl, I used to stand on the pier gazing out across the water, the salty wind ruffling my wavy red hair, stinging my deep green eyes with its harshness. The wind was as much a part of the seaside as the sand and the heat and the shells and the candyfloss. During my teenage years, I spent many nights frolicking on the beach with friends or else hanging around town and getting up to all kinds of mischief. As I reached adulthood, I never left the seaside behind, either physically or mentally, for it was and always shall be paradise.

At twenty-two, I still spent most of my free time on the beach. By that point, most of my friends had moved away. Some had gone to London to find their fortune, a couple had decided to backpack around the globe – two had even eloped to Peru, although I had no idea what was in Peru except for Paddington's aunt. I alone remained, for I had been born a child of the seaside and I had no intention of leaving it behind. There was no fortune in London worth the salt of the sea air; there was no place on the globe which could compare to the warm sunshine and heated beaches of the seaside; there was no love which could force me to elope, for it would mean surrendering my love of the place where my heart would always lie.

"How much is rock?"

I was jolted out of my daydream, for I had been staring out at the sea again. Working in an open-plan shop on the seafront, I could stare at the beach and sea all day if I wished. Fully one wall of the shop was missing – at night we lowered an iron grille to deter burglars – which invited the scent of the water and the biting winds to wash over me each and every day. It was a magical life and I would not have traded it for …

"Lady, the rock?"

"Sorry," I said. "Daydreaming again."

"You're daydreaming about me?"

I looked at the customer sceptically. He was here to surf, that much was obvious. His well-muscled legs were clutched tightly by black shorts which revealed something of the size of their content even though they masked it all. Other than the shorts, he was naked. His bronze torso glistened in the summer heat, his excessive time in the gym on display for all the girls to see. His face was boyish without being young, his hair was a scruffy styled mess which would have had most girls swooning.

"Sorry," I said with a professional smile. "Not my type. The rock's fifty pence a stick, three for a pound."

He selected three at random. "When do you get off work? We're having a little tournament later, you could come cheer me on."

"Sorry, I'm busy later. And, no offence, but you're really not my type."

He had not been the first guy to try to chat me up while at work and he would not be the last. I had learned the best way to deal with them was to keep smiling and keep repeating myself until they got the hint and went away. In the meantime, they would buy stuff. Some even returned to buy more stuff. I never led any of them on, would always tell them no, and eventually they would all get the message. My boss, Jasmine, didn't see any harm in it although told me to never actively lead anyone on because that would be cruel. I could not imagine being cruel to anyone and she said she knew but had to say so anyway.

Bosses are weird like that.

The shop itself was small, but well-packed with goods. We sold sticks of rock in three different sizes, as well as the novelty rock we had delivered. Toys, T-shirts and ornaments lined our shelves, while postcards stood on a swivel rack by the entrance. About the only thing we didn't stock were things with tiny seahorses stuck to them because those were real seahorses and that was cruel.

I noticed two boys over by the rubber dinosaurs. What dinosaurs had to do with the seaside, I had no idea, but it made my heart smile to watch them debate which of the toys they should buy.

"That's a cute smile," someone said.

I did not lose the smile, but I did inwardly sigh, for I had lost count of the number of times someone had used that line on me. As my eyes turned to my customer, however, my breath caught in my throat.

She was probably around thirty, so around eight years older than me. Her eyes were as blue as the ocean, her dark hair short and coarse, cut roughly by her own hands with a pair of scissors and a mirror. Parts of it stood almost like spikes, although I don't think she had put any thought to it. Her smile was playful, creating dimples in her cheeks, while she held her head lopsided as she regarded me. She was wearing blue shorts, revealing taut, muscular legs, and a loose white T-shirt, sweaty from the sun, showing bare and golden arms. Over her shoulder was slung a jacket, as though she really had not known what the weather was going to be like at the beach. It told me she was not a local, which likely meant she had come to the seaside for a holiday.

"I'll admit," she said, "I've never had someone completely ignore me before when I paid them a compliment."

"Sorry," I said, wishing I would stop daydreaming every two seconds. "Yes. I mean, thanks. You too."

"I too what?"

I took a deep breath. "Rowena."

"Cara." She extended her hand and I took it. She shook it once, hard, before releasing it. "Pleased to meet you."

"Yeah. Pleased."

"Do you have any Crocs?"

"Crocodiles?"

"Shoes."

"I know. It's a little joke I sometimes use."

"I can see why you call it a little joke."

There was nothing offensive about anything she was saying, for I could see there was humour to her eyes. That she was laughing at me would have been cruel, but it was more that she was playing. And I knew how to play with the best of them.

"We have similar sandals," I said, indicating the area where they were kept. "They're not Crocs, though. I think green would suit you."

"Green?" She pulled a face. "You seriously want me to wear green?"

"I like green."

"Then it's the first thing so far I don't like about you."

"So far?"

She moved off to the sandals without answering. I watched her try on a few pairs but was distracted when the two boys with their dinosaurs approached the till to buy what they had chosen. I complimented them on their choices, made a roaring noise with one, only to be told it was a herbivore, and the two boys happily departed the shop.

"You're good with kids," Cara said, depositing a pair of green sandals on the counter.

"So you went with green after all," I noted, my heart skipping a beat.

"They're the only ones that fit me properly. And comfort triumphs style. I'll bet you only have green in this size on purpose, just so you can get rid of old stock."

"You sound like a businesswoman."

"I dabble. I'm a photographer."

"Wow, that's interesting. Is that why you're at the beach?"

"Yep. There are some great scenic shots here, you just have to pick the right moment."

"Are you seeing anyone, Cara?"

"That's not picking the right moment, that's grabbing the bull by the horns."

I bit my lower lip, suitably chastised. I also feared I had ruined everything before it had begun. "Sorry, I tend to get a bit ahead of myself. I daydream a lot, it fills my head with fluff. That's what my mum used to say. My head's been filled with fluff my whole life. Like candyfloss, churning in that strange machine that makes it."

"Candyfloss is made by machine?"

"It's like that scene from Ghost. With the clay pot? That's what it always reminds me of, anyway."

"So," Cara said, "we've known each other two minutes and you've already asked me if I'm single and brought up one of the most iconic romantic scenes in film ever."

I tapped the side of my head. "Fluff."

Cara laughed. "No."

"No what?"

"No, I'm not seeing anyone. And no, I don't mind at all that you're bringing up that scene. You're a funny girl, Rowena."

"I've been called worse."

Another customer wanted serving and I tended to him quickly. Cara waited patiently.

"You have a knack for this sort of thing," she said once we were alone again – well, alone aside from the other people in the shop. "You have a wonderful smile that never fades."

"When I was born," I said, "no one told me smiles are like tides, so mine never goes away."

"The oddest thing anyone's ever said to me."

"My mother used to say that to me."

"Your mother sounds like a wise woman."

"Yeah, she was great."

"Sandals?"

"Oh, sorry." I told her how much they were and Cara paid in cash. "You want a bag for those?" I asked.

"For shoes? No, I'm going to wear them." She kicked off what she was wearing and slipped on the green sandals. "They still look horrendous," she said as she modelled them, "but I suppose crocodiles are green, so it makes sense for them to be this colour."

"They're not made of real crocodiles, you know."

"Yeah. I never thought they were."

I felt as though I had offended her, but she did not act offended.

"You're a local girl, right?" Cara asked.

"Born and raised."

"I need someone to show me around. I have a lot of work to be doing and could do with a guide to all the best places."

"I could so do that."

"I'd pay you, but I don't have two beans to rub together. Not that anyone would rub two beans together if they had them."

"No," I said. "They'd plant them and grow them into beanstalks."

"You do have an active imagination." She smiled again, which was a joy to see.

"If I'm going to be helping you," I said, my heart fluttering with nerves, "I should probably take your number."

"Are you allowed to ask for a customer's phone number, Rowena?"

"No. But rules are made to be broken."

"I wouldn't want to get you in trouble. It'd be a shame if you got sacked because I led you astray, I'd feel terrible."

"I don't mind taking the risk. Sometimes it's healthy to be led astray."

"I suppose it all depends on how much you enjoy the process."

My heart was about ready to explode with nerves but my boss chose that moment to appear. Jasmine Chakma was a short woman with large friendly eyes but a stern glower for anyone she didn't like. She had celebrated her thirty-first birthday a month earlier and I had my father help bake her a cake and everything. My dad made a living from his culinary masterpieces and always seized the opportunity to show off. Jasmine was a good employer but I could tell from her expression that this was one of her stern-glower moments.

"How's business?" Jasmine asked as she raised the bar of the counter and stood behind it with me. She opened a box and started sorting through some things which really didn't need sorting through.

"Fine," I said. "We made a few sales this morning, nothing major, though."

"I just bought some sandals," Cara said, twisting her feet to model them again.

"They look nice," Jasmine said with a smile. "Really suit you."

I looked to Cara, whose smile had vanished. She was uncomfortable with Jasmine there, although Jasmine was ignoring us both as she continued rummaging through her boxes.

"Anyway," Cara said, "must dash. I have to go test out these sandals. Thanks."

And she was gone. Gone from my life, just like that.

"How could you do that?" I asked, rounding upon Jasmine.

"Rowena, this is a business. The other customers don't want to watch you sorting out your love life. They want to buy stuff, and our job is to sell them stuff. Everyone wins if we just do our jobs."

Everyone wins, I thought, except me. I did not, of course, say anything of the sort.

I spent the next hour serving customers and picking up any stock people had dropped. Wandering around the shop, I kept surreptitiously looking up and down the promenade in case Cara was still hanging around, but there was no sign of her. Whenever I did that, I found Jasmine staring daggers at me, so I stopped.

At midday, Jasmine said I could take my lunch-break, so I headed down to the beach with my bag. I tended to spend my lunch there, for the sun did not affect me even during the hottest hours. Having grown up at the seaside, I had become immune to the sun's rays, or at least strengthened against them. In the height of summer, I would generally take a parasol with me, but I had been so anxious about Cara that day that I entirely forgot.

Near the shop was a place which sold ice cream and sandwiches, with a few tables and chairs outside. I watched the gulls eyeing the tables clinically, for seagulls are massive birds with a lot of power in them. I had seen them devour whole battered fish from someone's plate before and steal an ice cream from a man's hand. One of my schoolfriends who had moved to London e-mailed me one time to tell me the pigeons did the same thing in Oxford Street, but I was never convinced.

Reaching the beach, I kicked off my shoes and carried them to where I was going to sun myself and eat my lunch. The sand was hot underfoot, scorching in fact, for the summer was cruel, but I did not mind. There were a lot of people on the beach, dressed for the weather. Some children were chasing each other while their parents lazed in the sun; two old men had their deck-chairs out; a few teenagers frolicked in the surf, playing some game where they avoided the surf when in actual fact it just gave them an opportunity to shove each other. Everyone was having fun, for that was what the beach was all about.

Finding a spot away from any ball games, I settled down, realising I had forgotten even to bring a towel to lie on. I was wearing loose trousers and a shirt, but that was because I had been at work. Beneath these I always wore my bikini, and had no problem slipping off the clothes. I used my shirt as a towel to sit on as I applied suntan lotion down my arms and legs. I was always amazed by how many people avoided sunblock, only to burn afterwards. My application routine took around five minutes, which I was told was short but, since I did it so often, I had it down to an art form. My neck, my cleavage, the backs of my ears – nothing was safe from my rubbing fingers. Having red hair, I was one of those girls whose skin was naturally pale, but spending so long in the sun had brought the life out in my skin and I was always proud of the warm glow it seemed to have.

Putting my suntan lotion back in my bag, I pulled out my bottle of water and my foil-wrapped sandwiches. Balling my shirt into a pillow, I dropped my sunglasses over my eyes and stared out at the sea. The waves were intense that day, as though they wanted to join the game the teenagers were playing and soak them as much as possible. In the distance, I could spy a yacht and wondered whether the people on board were looking towards the beach and thinking of all the people there.

I thought again of Cara. Throughout my lunch-time routines, I had managed to forget about her, but while I lay there contemplating things, her face returned to my thoughts. I understood what Jasmine meant, for I was at work and there had to be rules, but she could at least have let me get Cara's number. Now there was some gorgeous dark-haired beauty walking around in green sandals she didn't even like, alone because Jasmine wouldn't let me talk to her for two more minutes.

I was not angry with Jasmine. I knew I probably should have been, but she was only looking out for the shop. Business had not been too good lately and if sales did not start picking up soon, we were going to close down.

Still ... two minutes.

Staring at my foil-wrapped sandwiches, I found I had lost my appetite. Plus, I had left them out in the sun too long and now the heat would be baking the foil and the sandwiches within.

I took a sip of water, but even that was against me because it had already turned warm.

It was when I realised I had forgotten my hat that I decided it had been the worst day ever.

"Mind if I join you?"

I looked up to find Cara standing a few feet away. She was dressed as she had been when I had last seen her, sandals and all. I could not believe what I was seeing and knew I must have been daydreaming all over again. Raising myself onto my elbows, I stared at her through my sunglasses. Her smile was the same as before, although the playfulness in her eyes was a little wilder. I put it down to our location, for on the beach there was no one who could tell us what we could and couldn't do. Within reason, of course.

"That a yes or a no?" she asked.

"Yes. Sorry, yes, yes, oh yes."

"Not a creepy answer at all," Cara said as she sat beside me. She did not at all hide the way she cast her eyes across my body and as she found my eyes, her face was aglow. "You're a difficult woman to pin down, Rowena."

"And I'm the one with the creepy remarks?" I asked.

"Touché. That boss of yours is a bit of a grouch. She needs to learn to have some fun once in a while."

"Jasmine? She's just worried about the business."

"Not good?"

I shrugged. "I'd rather talk about you. You're a photographer? That's amazing."

"It'd be more amazing if I could make some decent money out of it, but thanks for saying so."

"Still want me to show you around?"

"Absolutely, if you're up for it. We never finished our chat. You've lived in Glazton your whole life?"

"I'm lucky enough that my father owns a house overlooking the sea."

"Must be expensive. Your father loaded?"

"No, my parents got some deal on it years ago. I don't understand all that sort of thing, but then I don't have my own place."

"You live with your folks?"

I felt as though she was judging me. I was only twenty-two, I was allowed to live with my father.

She must have seen my reaction because she said, "Hey, if I could still live with my folks, I'd be back home like a shot. Living on your own is expensive. You're, what? Twenty?"

"Twenty-two."

"Wow, that's the sea air for you."

Everything she said was perfect and I tried to think of something witty to say, something which might have impressed her. Instead, I lay there saying nothing again.

"I get the vibe that your mother's not on the scene any more," Cara said.

"She died when I was twelve. Cancer."

"I'm sorry."

"It's been ten years. I'm not going to say it doesn't still hurt, but I can't dwell on what happened."

"My folks don't talk to me."

"Because you're gay?"

"No, because they hate me."

"That's horrible." I could not imagine anyone hating their child – I certainly could not imagine anyone ever hating Cara.

"What time do you get off?" she asked.

"Whenever you're ready."

"Work. What time do you get off work?"

I was glad of the sunglasses because I flushed crimson in that moment. If only I could have blamed it on the sun, but Cara seemed to find it funny. "Seven," I said.

"You do long shifts."

"Like I said, we need the money. Jasmine doesn't have any other staff, so it's just the two of us."

"What are you having for dinner tonight?"

"My dad's cooking fish."

She wrinkled her nose. "Shame. I was going to ask you to meet me in a bar, but it can wait."

"No, no," I said too quickly, wondering why I was presenting an image to this older woman that I was some kid who had to go home to her father every night. "It's just fish – I can meet you."

"You sure? I don't want to start things off between us by annoying your dad. Who knows? I might get to meet him one day."

I was glad I was lying down, because my knees went weak first from the thought of starting a relationship and second from the thought of her meeting my father. But I breathed deeply, for I was getting ahead of myself. Cara was just talking, she didn't mean anything. If I was right and she was around thirty, she would have far more experience than I did with relationships. The last thing I wanted to come across as was naïve or young.

"I'll call home, it's fine," I said. "Dad keeps telling me I need to go out more."

"Liking your father now as well."

"So, bar?"

"There's one on the pier. *The Mermaid*. Although, last I checked, there weren't any mermaids there."

"They have a mermaid theme."

"I know. I only went there because I thought there'd be a lot of hot girls dressed for the occasion, but to be honest the whole experience was a bit of a let-down."

"The food's good."

"Then I'll buy you dinner."

"Fantastic. Meet you at just after seven?"

"If you get off at seven, you'll need to go home, right? Shower and change and whatever? Meet me at eight."

I didn't need to go home to shower and change, but I had been perspiring heavily since Cara had appeared on the beach so I wondered whether I stank of sweat. I desperately wanted to take a sniff under my arms to check, but that would have been a sure way to send Cara running.

"Eight o'clock," I said in agreement.

"Great. Sorted, then. See you at eight."

She walked off, her green sandals looking really odd now that I could see her wearing them on the beach. But she was still wearing them, which told me she valued my opinion.

Lying back on my makeshift pillow, I gazed up at the deep blue sky and released a heavy sigh. I was too nervous to eat so lay there thinking of the wonderful evening ahead of me. I would have to phone my father at some point to tell him I had a date, but was still not sure whether to tell him that much.

With a stab of remorse, I realised I had again failed to secure Cara's phone number and had probably had the perfect opportunity to get it. Still, if things went well, I would have it by the end of the night.

After that, I imagined our relationship would blossom into something beautiful.

I spent the remainder of my lunch-break lost in wonderful daydreams about the possibility of having just found my perfect woman.

# CHAPTER TWO

I had not told my father that I had a date that night, but it was pretty obvious to him. When I got home from work, I went immediately to my bedroom and started throwing clothes onto my bed. My father left me to it and my sister helped me pick out something suitable. I was all for wearing a dress, but my sister cautioned me against that and told me I should definitely be more casual. I suggested the tightest trousers I had and she just laughed at me.

As I arrived at the pier, I was therefore wearing blue jeans, trainers, a light blue T-shirt and a thin brown jacket. I considered tying my hair back into a ponytail, but my sister again disagreed and told me I should wear it loose and free. My hair was not exactly curly, but it was far from straight and she always said it was my best feature.

"Ro," she had said, "this girl you're seeing tonight will be dreaming about your hair."

The wind on the pier caught my hair, bouncing it but not ruffling it too badly, and I felt my confidence grow. My stomach was still turning at the thought of meeting Cara again, but at least I knew I looked my best.

I felt a little bad for my family, for I had told them nothing about Cara. My father had not pressed, but my sister always loved to gossip about such things. I had told them only that I had met a girl at work, that she was dark-haired and had a quirky smile. I had not told them Cara was around eight years or so older than me, for I knew my father would not approve. He would not have insisted I take my sister as a chaperone (despite her being a year younger than me), but he would have cautioned me, and I had not wanted to worry him.

The pier was filled with people, all of them having a good time. The pier of Glazton was a grand affair, filled with arcades, rides and vendors. There was a big wheel to take you to the heavens, a ghost train to take you to the Underworld, a shooting gallery to show off to your friends and bars where you could make new ones.

Over the years, I had tried everything the pier had to offer. Sometimes I had been alone, at other times I had been with friends, and I had spent more than a few dates there. With my friends having moved away, I had not visited the pier as much as I had when I was younger, but I enjoyed it none the less.

The ghost train was where I had held hands with Suzie, the rollercoaster was where I had shrieked with Max and Freda, the candyfloss stall was where Jackie, Suzie and I had accepted the boys' challenge of eating as much as we could. There were also bad memories: throwing up behind the doughnut stall, being slapped by Liz when she thought I'd kissed her girlfriend, getting drunk and kissing Liz's girlfriend.

Glazton was full of memories for me and it was with some sadness that I realised every one of those people had moved away.

I moved through the crowds, all the bright lights and sounds an ordinary occurrence to me. Being summer, eight o'clock did not bring complete darkness, but that did not stop the rides from flashing their blazing lights, enticing customers into their grasp.

Ordinarily, I would have been enjoying everything along the way, but I was too nervous to engage in any of it. *The Mermaid* was a bar at the end of the pier, although why anyone thought putting a bar on the end of a pier was a good idea, I'll never know. During my late-teenage years, I spent so many nights in that place. As with the pier itself, it was filled with memories both good and bad. It was where I got into a blazing argument with Harry about pizza, where I watched George and Suzie get together (which was terrible, because I'd had my eye on Suzie ever since we held hands on the rollercoaster). It was also where I had met Lauren, who had been my first real love, my first real kiss. I remembered every detail of that night. Our friends had pushed us together because they saw we kept looking at each other and looking away. We spoke all night, held hands, sat on the comfy chairs and kissed for over an hour. Looking back, I was surprised the bar staff hadn't turfed us out for that. It was also the night I would have lost my virginity, except we both decided to wait, not wanting to push things too far too quickly.

I stepped inside to find *The Mermaid* the same familiar location it had always been, but then it had only been about a month since I had last been there. It had changed some since I was a teenager, but only in basic aesthetics. I wondered how much of that was my own perception, and whether it was possible the bar could have remained the same since the day it opened.

There were twelve tables in *The Mermaid* and most were already taken. The bar was busy with customers, mainly teenagers, although there were families who had stopped by, too. There were shells of every size painstakingly fixed to the walls, along with a ship's wheel and an anchor. There were representations of starfish, too, and paintings of other fish I couldn't name. I had once held a summer job at *The Mermaid* and had come to understand how annoying it was to keep the place dusted.

Strolling to the bar, I managed to get served fairly quickly, mainly because I knew the people who worked there. There were three staff behind the bar that night, and I was lucky enough to have Sophie opposite me. Sophie was in her forties and had been there the night I had spent making out with Lauren that time. It was Sophie I had to thank for not kicking me out; she had always been there to look out for me.

I ordered a lemonade and Sophie fired it into a glass.

"It's been a while, Ro," she said.

"Work, you know how it is."

"I certainly do. You alone tonight?"

"I'm meeting someone."

"Someone special?"

"Mmm, not sure yet."

She smiled as she passed over my drink and I paid for it. "Let me know if you want me to change the music."

I had not even noticed the music. It was soft, unobtrusive, and I had a sudden horror of Sophie playing something deeply romantic, like that song they played over the pottery scene in Ghost. I could not at that moment think of the song, but it would have destroyed me.

"Ro, calm down," Sophie said with a frown. "I'm not really going to do anything. Are you all right?"

"Just nervous."

"Been there myself more than once. Anyone I know?"

"I doubt it. She's not from around here."

"Ooh, a holiday romance. Well, take care not to get burned, Ro. A lot of these holiday-makers are only after one thing. People think it's just the guys looking for that, but women can be just as bad."

"Thanks, Soph, but I'm always careful."

She pulled a wry face, not agreeing with me but being diplomatic enough not to say as much aloud. "Still, maybe I should get Frank out here anyway."

I laughed. Frank was *The Mermaid*'s one-man security force. He was also Sophie's husband and the sweetest man I had ever met. He may have been big, bald and scarred, but he also loved to knit and had the sexiest singing voice I had ever heard.

Moving over to one of the last remaining tables, I sat with my drink and waited.

Ten minutes later, Sophie wandered by with a cloth to wipe down the tables. The tables always needed wiping down, but that was not the reason for her to have come over. I could see the concern in her face, but I put on a brave smile regardless.

"I'm early," I said.

"What time are you meeting?"

I glanced at my watch. It was already quarter past eight, so I said, "Half eight."

"OK. You want another drink?"

"I'm good, thanks."

"OK."

She walked off to wipe down another table.

Twenty minutes later, she was back again. I smiled, although said nothing. I felt foolish as well as nervous, and my embarrassment must have burned my face. I could not believe I had told Sophie why I was there. I should have told her I had come to the bar so I could sit at a table for half an hour, drinking the same glass of lemonade.

"Maybe she's running late," Sophie said. "Have you called her?"

"She'll be here."

"You want me to call her?"

"No, thanks."

"You want Frank to call her?"

That broke a little of my nervousness. "I don't have her number."

"Ah."

"She's coming, Soph."

"I'm sure. It's just, if she doesn't, Ro, it's her loss, all right?"

"She hasn't stood me up."

"Not saying she has. She's probably just running late, like you said. I'm just saying you're a catch, Ro. If she can't see that, forget her."

"She's coming," I said through gritted teeth. "She's running late."

She smiled, said nothing and wiped the table for good measure.

I tried not to keep looking at the door, but it was difficult. It was while I was brooding into my lemonade that someone said, "This seat taken?"

I looked up to find a twenty-year-old guy with tanned, dark features and piercing brown eyes. Behind him, some way off, I saw three men of a similar age. They were pretending not to be watching us, but it was obvious they were waiting to see how their friend got on with me.

"Sorry," I said, "I'm waiting for someone."

"Maybe I've arrived."

"Maybe she's running late."

"Your sister? If she's half the vision you are, she's welcome to join us."

"I'm not waiting for my sister. No offence, because I'm sure you're a nice guy and all, but I really am waiting for someone. And you're not her."

He took that as an invitation to sit down. "Let me buy you a drink."

"No, thank you."

"Dinner?"

I did not like to think about it, but my stomach, as nervous as it was, was also famished. I had expected to be dining with Cara and it was already coming up to nine. I almost glanced at my watch, but that would have been rude. Why I was concerned with how rude the man who had just sat uninvited opposite me thought I was, I had no idea.

"No, thank you," I repeated.

"I just hate to see a pretty girl lonely."

"I'm not lonely. Don't take this the wrong way, but would you please go away?"

He laughed at this, as though it was a challenge. "My friends and I are down from Coventry. We ..."

"I don't care. Seriously, just go away." I did not mean to be rude, but with some people it was all they understood. Plus, my nerves were all but cracking and I was both angry and upset and if I was going to talk much more I would start crying.

He seemed to get the message, because he stood up without a word and went back to his friends. He laughed as he reached them, said something derogatory about me and they wandered off to the other side of the bar.

"You want me to have Frank kick them out?" Sophie asked as she returned to wipe my table down again.

"Would you please stop doing that?"

"Sorry. Just worried for you."

"I don't need anyone being worried about me, Soph." I glanced to the door one final time. "Maybe I should just go home. Dad was doing fish tonight."

"You mean you haven't eaten yet? Ro, you must be half starved. Let me get you something."

"I was supposed to be having dinner with Cara."

"Cara, eh? Well, she's an idiot for not being here. I can get you some fish, I'll even buy it for you."

"Soph, thanks, but I don't think I could eat right now. My stomach's barely holding this lemonade in and ..." I took a deep breath to stop myself from crying and wiped my eyes savagely. "Why do people do this, Soph? Why would someone get my hopes up and then ... She's probably not even gay. She's probably like that guy from Coventry. Had some fun with me and then went back to her mates to laugh about it."

"She's the one who's missing out, Ro." She slipped into the chair beside me and gave me a hug. She was warm and cosy, like a woman should be, although it was mainly on account of how hard she was working. "If I was half my age and into girls, I'd give my right arm to meet you in a bar, Ro."

"You're sweet, Soph," I said, wiping my eyes and trying not to cry again. "I should go home. Oh, I can't go home. My father will shake his head sadly and my sister will push me for details."

"Well you can't sit at this table all night."

"Could I give you a hand behind the bar?"

"Ro, stop it. Your father is a wonderful man. He'll give you better hugs than I can and he'll understand. He'll even cook you some fish, you'll see."

I sniffed and took another deep breath. "You're right. I should go."

"Rowena, sorry I'm late."

My heart thudded as Cara slipped into the chair opposite. She looked just the same as she had when I had last seen her – even her T-shirt was the same, so she had likely not been back home to change. The only difference was that she was no longer wearing the green sandals, for I had caught a flash of trainers under the table.

"It's fine," I said. "I got tied up with work anyway so I haven't been waiting long."

"Hi," Sophie said a little icily for my tastes. "You must be Cara."

"Yeah; and you?"

"This is Sophie," I said. "She works here."

"Is hugging the customers a part of the job description?"

"Only the customers I've known for years," Sophie said.

"Great. Get us two martinis."

"Ro doesn't drink."

Cara looked at me strangely. "No one doesn't drink. I thought you said you were twenty-two."

"I am twenty-two," I said. "But, no, I don't drink."

"Well, I'm not going to be drinking alone. Two martinis."

"One martini," Sophie said, "and a lemonade. I think the one she has ran its course a while back."

"It's fine, Soph," I said. "One won't hurt me."

"No," Sophie agreed, "because you're having a lemonade."

She moved off to fetch the drinks and Cara gazed at her with an amused expression. "And I thought *I* was a little old for you."

"Sophie's my friend. She looks out for me."

"Mothers you, more like. Why don't you drink?"

"I just don't."

"But why? I can't imagine not drinking. Listen to me, I sound like an alcoholic. You had a bad experience?"

"No, I've just never done it."

"Never?"

"No drink, no drugs."

"Wow, I'll bet you're a fun date."

Her flippancy was getting to me, but it was not making me angry like perhaps it should have. Instead, it was making me self-conscious and I feared I may have to do a few things I did not want to just to please this woman.

The drinks came a moment later – a martini and a lemonade – and Sophie handed us both menus.

"No time for food, sorry," Cara said. "It's after nine and I need to get back to my studio sharpish. Besides, I grabbed something about an hour ago."

"An hour ago?" Sophie asked. "You mean around eight?"

I glowered at Sophie, wishing she would mind her own business. I knew full well my stomach had been grumbling since I'd arrived at eight and that I had been waiting for Cara to show up; and I fully understood that while I was doing that, Cara was off eating something. I should have eaten something myself, it was hardly Cara's fault that I hadn't. Sophie had even offered me something to eat and I had turned it down.

Cara said something marginally pleasant and Sophie left us alone. She sipped her martini and said, "For a fairy godmother, your friend makes a decent martini."

I was not sure how exactly one made a martini, since I thought it came out of a bottle, but I did not say anything. "So," I said instead, "how's your day been?"

She shrugged. "Still trying to piece together all my shots. That was what delayed me. The studio I work out of? Some guy next door was helping me with my equipment and he wasn't going to be there forever so I had to grab him while I could."

"I understand. It's fine."

"What's fine?"

"You being late."

"Even if I did get here on time, you wouldn't have been here anyway, so it all worked out well."

"You said you need my help finding the best locations for shooting?"

"Yes. That's precisely what I need you for." She shot me a dazzling smile. "Sorry, it wasn't just a pretence to get to see you outside of work. Oh, I'm such a cow. You must think I'm using you."

I shrugged a little meekly.

"Hon, I'm sorry, I've just had a rough day. Yes, of course I want you to help me set up the scenic shots, but you're still cute as sin and I'm here because I want to be here."

It made me happy to hear her say that, although some of the fluttering had left my heart. I had to remind myself Cara was older than me, more experienced, with far more pressure in her job.

"Tell me about yourself," I said. "Your work sounds amazing."

"It pays the bills, or at least it would if I could get enough of it."

"It must be great to be freelance."

"It means I have a lot of bosses and no steady income. There are people who make a fortune doing what I do. Not me, though. You sure I can't tempt you?"

I flushed, uncertain what to say.

She raised her martini and I understood.

"I'm good," I said.

She continued talking as though she had not paused. "I do mainly scenic shots, some animal photography, which is insanely difficult. Most of the time it means sitting in a hut for days or under a tree or something, and still never getting the shot. Makes me so angry when some random chump snaps off a shot of a squirrel leaping out of a tree for a fallen nut and everyone goes crazy about it."

"You're very passionate about your work, Cara."

"If you're not passionate about something, it's not worth doing. You a virgin, by the way?"

The question threw me. "That's not something to ask a girl on the first date."

"Sorry, I just don't waste my time with virgins, and if you don't drink alcohol I reckon you might be prissy about sex as well."

Her way with words was uncouth, but she was not a woman who did anything slowly. I imagined her life was rapid-fire, what with taking thousands of photos, meeting deadlines and everything.

"None of my business, sorry," she said. Then she actually stopped a moment. "You're right, that was an inappropriate question for a first date. This *is* a date, right? This isn't just two friends meeting in a bar?"

I was struggling to keep up. "I saw it as a date."

"Great." She flashed a smile. "Have you ever gone down?"

"I ..." That was as far as I got before my mouth grew too dry to speak.

"The pier," she said, pointing at the floor. "Where it's dark and gungy. If we get there at sunset, I reckon I'll be able to take some fantastic shots. Do you have crabs?"

"On the beach?" I ventured.

"Yeah. Some crabs in the shot would be good, too. Is it your time of the month?"

I was beginning to suspect she was toying with me. "For what?"

"Tides."

At last, I relaxed, for I understood her game. "The tides aren't monthly, they're twice daily. This time of year, low tide is about nine o'clock, high tide is around three."

"Caught me out. Still, twice daily has to be better than once a month."

"You know," I said, taking a sip of lemonade, "I still don't get you. One moment I think you're the worst influence I could ever meet, the next I see a fun side to you."

"Yeah, I play around a lot. Well, when I say play around a lot, I don't mean like that. I mean I like to have fun with words. Innuendo's kind of my thing. It helps in my line of work."

"How?"

"I take a photo of a car, someone has to comment on it having a nice body. I take a photo of a bird, someone has to mention tit, even though it's clearly an albatross. That sort of thing. All the while, I have to stand on the other side of the desk, holding my tongue in the hope they're going to buy some photos."

"That must be hard."

She shrugged, leaned more comfortably on her chair and finished her martini. "What's the time?"

"You don't have a watch?"

"If I had a watch, I wouldn't have been late."

I looked at my wrist. "Five and twenty to ten."

"Five and twenty to ten?" she laughed. "You sure you're twenty-two? My grandmother talks like that."

I felt uncomfortable with her laughing at me and glanced to the bar to see Sophie staring at her with narrowed eyes. Cara did not appear to have noticed at all and I was having a difficult time reconciling the woman opposite me with the one I had flirted with back at the shop.

"You know what?" Cara said, "I've finished my drink and this place is a dive. What say we hit the pier?"

"The pier?"

"You can show me the best rides and stuff. I'll even buy you an ice cream."

"That sounds fantastic."

"Ease off, it's just a pier." She got up and headed for the door without me. Rising myself, I made off after her, but Sophie was beside me in an instant.

"Ro, that's your date?"

"Yes," I said defiantly, not prepared to be lectured. The truth was, Cara was not what I had expected and I did not need Sophie's opinion on the matter.

"Ro, just be careful, all right? Promise me you won't let things get too far."

"How do you mean?"

"You're a sweet girl, but Cara's a traveller. She's here for the sights and the experiences. You're a sight but I don't want you to become an experience."

"I'm not an experience," I said heatedly, "and my love life is none of your business."

"I know. Just don't lose your head."

Sophie meant well, but it was not what I wanted to hear. I left *The Mermaid* and hurried to catch up to Cara. I did not know what the night would bring, but it was no one's business but ours. The evening belonged to us, and I would do whatever I pleased.

# CHAPTER THREE

The pier closed late in the summer and at night it was an explosion of sound and light, intensified by the darkness. Evening on the pier was a different world to anything I had ever known and there were so many people doing so many things it was difficult to know where to begin. Some of the places had shut up early, for they were family-oriented and most families would have been back in their hotels by quarter to ten.

We stopped by the railing for a while and watched as lifeguards hared off to rescue someone, their speedboat roaring like a lion on a mission.

"Why's anyone swimming at this hour?" Cara asked.

"It's probably a drunk. They fall in from time to time. They cause no end of problems for the lifeguards."

"People fall in the sea when they're drunk? Why do they put a bar on the pier, then? Drown your sorrows then drown yourself."

"That's not funny. Our lifeguards do a fantastic job and people need to appreciate them more."

"I just think anyone stupid enough to fall in the sea after drinking deserves to drown."

"That's harsh. What about the people who jump?"

"If life's so bad that you have to jump in the sea, then you should just die and get it over with."

"I can't believe you just said that."

She shrugged, clearly not much caring what my opinion was. As the lifeboat disappeared into the black and shining distance of the sea, Cara and I wandered around the pier. I pointed out all the best places to visit and the most exciting games to play.

We stopped at a shooting gallery and Cara held the rifle as though she knew precisely what she was doing. Her first shot struck the piled cans dead centre, but her second missed entirely. We moved onto a hoopla stall, where I tried and failed to win something; and then we found we were really rubbish at throwing a basketball into a hoop barely larger than the ball itself.

For the next half hour or so, we played games and spent a little money here and there. Cara was fun to be with, but she never once initiated any contact with me. I did not know how to behave around her. When I'd had girlfriends in the past, I'd always found they thrilled from the barest touch just as much as I did, but Cara was more interested in playing the games than who she was playing them with.

It was because of this that I suggested we go on the rollercoaster, since we would have to hold hands or something while we were up there.

"Nah, I don't do rollercoasters," she said. "They remind me too much of real life. What's that over there?"

"Crazy golf."

"Crazy gold? On a pier? Are you people nuts? Hey look, bumper cars."

There was indeed a cordoned-off area where six small one-person cars, each of different colours, sat waiting for customers. It was not a busy place and presently there was no one in any of the cars.

"Quick, get us some tokens," Cara said as she headed over to tell the man we wanted two cars.

I paid for the tokens at a booth and took them over to the man running the ride. They were not cheap – seaside tokens are never cheap – and spending them on bumper cars was not quite the evening I had imagined. Bumper cars were perhaps the least intimate ride on the whole pier and I wanted to tell her that, but I didn't want to upset her.

Cara chose a red car and I sat in a green one. The man ran through the basics with us, made sure our seat belts were tight, and activated the power. Lights appeared on each car and they moved along by use of a steering wheel. There were no pedals, but then I supposed there was no point in adding brakes to a bumper car.

I was just trying to get the hang of the steering when Cara's red car thumped mine in the side.

"Hey," I said.

"It's the game, sweetie," she said with a laugh, veering around for another pass.

"I always get bumper cars mixed up with dodgems," I said.

"They're the same thing. One's just the name wusses use."

She came at me again and I spun the wheel to evade her but didn't manage to move in time. Her car struck me at the back and I jolted forward. Spinning my wheel, I tried to get around her, but she was good at controlling her car and thumped me in the side before I could do anything.

Laughing, she circled me, leaning back with joy, and came directly for me. I spun the wheel again, but she countered my every move and slammed the nose of her car into mine in a head-on collision. I jolted so hard the straps keeping me in chafed and I grimaced.

The ride did not last much longer and when I clambered out of the car, I felt like I had just paid to get beaten up.

"You're terrible at that," Cara said, still laughing. "For a native, you clearly haven't done that before."

"I tend to like less violent games," I said, rubbing my sore legs.

"That's because you're boring."

My face fell and I was suddenly seeing the truth to what Sophie had warned me about.

"Hey, why so sad?" Cara asked. "I don't mean that in a bad way. You've just been living in a shell all your life, Ro. You know what? I don't even know your surname."

"Shelby."

"Shelby? After I just said you've been living in a shell? That's too rich."

"What about you?" I asked.

"What about me what?"

"Your surname."

"Hughes. Not nearly as dramatic as Miss Shelby who lives by the sea. Oh, you're kidding me."

"Kidding you?"

"Shelby sells seashells by the seashore. Because that's what you do. You can't make this stuff up."

"Stop laughing at me."

She stopped laughing and tilted her head. "You need to lighten up, Ro."

"I'm trying, but you're making it very difficult."

Her demeanour changed at once. Gone was the cocksure firebrand and in her eyes shone concern for my well-being. She took me by the hands and held them. It was our first physical contact and it sent waves of conflicting emotions through me. I was still angry and upset, but could not deny the thrill which almost convulsed my body.

"I'm sorry," she said. "I get like this sometimes. I find it difficult to get out of work mode, since it where I'm most comfortable."

"You're not comfortable with me?"

"I'm ... nervous."

"You? You're not nervous."

"Are you kidding, Ro? I meet a gorgeous redhead with green eyes and a fantastic smile. I flirt with her, she flirts with me and we agree to go on a date. She's years younger than me and could have any girl she wanted, even a few who think they're straight. But for some reason she wants to spend time with me? Why wouldn't I be nervous about that?"

It had never occurred to me that Cara's attitude was all a front, that she was just as anxious about our date as I was. I tightened my grip on her hands and said, "Let's start again. We can try something else, something that doesn't involve attacking each other in vehicles."

"Deal."

We spent the remainder of the night enjoying the games we had not tried, but this time we played them together. We even managed to win a small teddy, but it was on the hook-a-duck and everyone wins at hook-a-duck. Cara wanted me to keep it but I insisted she did. She asked me to sign the bear's shirt, which was the oddest thing a date had ever asked me to do, but I was happy to. Cara said it was so the bear would forever belong to the both of us, which, as romantic gestures went, I still found a little strange.

Not having eaten, I was spending far too much energy so we had doughnuts and candyfloss, which were probably not the most nutritious things we could have had. Cara then bought me that ice cream she had promised and it was wonderful.

Next, we visited the amusement arcade. It was rare for the arcade to be open that late, but in summer Glazton tended not to close until everyone was done having fun. The arcade was a dazzling display of lights and music, and we found some plastic horses to bet on for ten pence each. I chose the green horse and it came in to win me a little profit.

"Maybe there's something to liking green after all," Cara said.

I asked Cara whether we could try our luck at the claw machines but she pulled a face.

"That's kids' stuff, Rowena."

Ever since coming off the bumper cars, I had been more relaxed, yet her words made me self-conscious all over again about our age difference. I had been worried about my father thinking Cara was too old for me, yet there were also concerns in my head that Cara would herself consider me too young. Her earlier words had given me confidence, for to think of her as nervous herself was encouraging, even if that did make me a bad person for feeling that way.

"What do you want to do, then?" I asked, hoping there was something in the arcade which would attract her attention.

She looked around. "There's a photo booth. We could get some shots done."

"Sure."

The booth was slightly larger than one you would find in a high-street shop. It was not designed to take passport photos, but for groups of people to get in so they could have a laugh. It was still a tight fit just to get the two of us in together, but back when I was a teenager I think my friends and I set a record for managing to squeeze eleven people in. Getting out had proved something of an issue, but it had been a memorable experience.

There was a small bench inside rather than the swivel chair one would find in the passport-photo booths, and Cara sat on it first. I squeezed in and was acutely aware that our bodies were closer than they had been all night. Our sides pressing up against each other, I could feel the heat from Cara's body and breathed in her scent. If she was wearing any perfume, it had not been applied recently and indeed I doubted she had even showered before coming out for our date. The seaside heat was always powerful and there were times in the past where I had taken three showers in the span of one day.

A lot of little things were adding up to making me wonder just how committed Cara was to our relationship. She had claimed to be nervous, yet at times she acted downright uncaring. I began to question whether she was right for me, whether I would want to see her again. It had been a while since

I had been on a date and I could not forget the magic at our first meeting. We had shared something during our flirting and I was not about to allow that to disappear entirely without trying to rekindle it.

"Can you reach the buttons?" Cara asked and I realised I had been daydreaming again.

Reaching over, I pressed the button to take the picture and we both grinned like fools until the flash shone through the booth. I looked to Cara, whose face was close to mine, and I wondered how she would react should I move in to kiss her.

"Show's over, Ro; let's go get our picture."

The moment passed and I slipped out of the booth, Cara coming after me. The photograph was printed on paper which came out the side. It was done in a strange pencil effect, as though there was someone very small inside the booth drawing away. When it emerged, it looked rather odd, but at least we both looked happy.

"You want it?" I asked.

"Nah, I got the bear. You take the photo."

I was glad she had said that, because I most certainly did want the photo. Wishing I had somewhere to keep it without having to fold it, I tucked it away in the back pocket of my jeans and hoped it would not become too creased.

An announcement came over the public address system to say the arcade would be closing in ten minutes. I had not realised so much time had passed and did not want the evening to end.

Leaving the arcade, we walked out into the brisk winds of the seaside evening and strolled back down the pier towards the town. Cara had her hands in her pockets and I longed to hold one of those hands but was too nervous to ask and was certainly not brazen enough to slip my hand into her pocket with them.

"Tonight's certainly been an eye-opener," Cara said. "Thanks for the date, Ro. It's been fun, hasn't it?"

"Yeah." We stopped as we left the pier and faced each other. "Listen, I have work tomorrow, but we should meet up again real soon. I still have to show you the best sights."

"Work, yeah." She shuddered at the thought. "I have so much to do and I still don't have any decent shots of Glazton. I'll drop by and see you tomorrow. When's the dragon not there?"

"Jasmine's not a dragon."

"You sure? I was certain I saw her breathe fire."

"She's not so bad. I don't really know what time she'll be around, but just take a chance."

"Life's all about taking chances, Ro."

My heart was thumping terribly by this point and my lips were dry. As I gazed into Cara's eyes, I desperately wanted to kiss her but still had no idea how she would react if I tried. Her attitude was so strange, I still could not understand her, and trying to predict her would have been useless.

I decided to take the chance, for that was clearly what she had meant. Leaning in, I tilted my head and parted my lips, but Cara drew back.

"Whoa, Ro, not so fast."

I dropped back to my feet, having gone to tiptoe as I leaned forward. I felt embarrassed at the rejection, but she was not offended. In fact, she was smiling that lopsided smile of hers. I didn't know what to say, so said nothing.

"Not that we're not going there eventually," she said. "It's just I make it a rule never to kiss on a first date. Sorry, I'm just that kind of girl."

"No worries," I said. "I can wait. Does this mean we're having a second date, where we *can* kiss?"

"I'd like that. But I also have to do a lot of work tomorrow. No offence, but if I want to eat, I have to meet my deadlines and everything else gets sidelined when I have deadlines."

I did not like to think that I was being sidelined, but understood work commitments well enough. "Tomorrow, then," I said.

"Sure. Tomorrow." For a moment, it looked as though she was about to say or do something else; then she pulled her jacket a bit tighter against the wind and walked off. I watched her go, desperately wishing she had let me kiss her, yet still feeling embarrassed and more than a little confused. I liked her and I thought she liked me, yet nothing of note had happened on our first date. We had had fun, or at least I thought we had, although as I walked home in the chilly town air, I reflected that perhaps I just wanted to believe I'd had fun.

I hoped by the time I got home, my sister and father would be in bed. If either of them should have asked me how my date had gone, I was far too confused to give them any kind of honest answer.

# CHAPTER FOUR

Jasmine was at the shop all morning and I just wished she would leave. She spent most of it stocktaking and, while she did not say anything, she was not happy with our sales. She would never lie to me about our financial situation, but she did tend to keep things from me. I knew she was looking out for me, but it seemed everyone did that. My father, Sophie, Jasmine ... it was no wonder I had drifted to someone who sometimes feigned indifference.

We had mainly browsers in the shop that morning, with a few sales scattered about. I kept an eye out for Cara, but as the morning drew to an end, there had been no sign of her. On the one hand, I was pleased, for if she should turn up when Jasmine was present, I would be in for it. On the other hand, I was mortified Cara had forgotten me, that she had found something better to be doing with her time. Thankfully, my sister had been in bed by the time I had got home the night before, and my father had not asked too many questions. Nor had Jasmine asked anything of Cara, but that was because she did not know I had been to the pier with her.

At around midday, Jasmine finally sat on a box behind the counter with me and swigged from a bottle of water. There were only two customers in the shop at the time and both of those were browsers, so I was able to talk with her.

"You look sad, boss."

"It's summer, Rowena. We should be doing ten times better than we are."

"It's the places that opened by the arcades, right?"

She nodded. Last summer, a shop similar to ours had opened on the main road, right next to the biggest arcades. Competition was fine, and had never much affected us before. Everyone coming to the beach wanted trinkets and needed beach-balls, so all the shops tended to do well. Being situated on the seafront, our trade in footwear and beach toys always vastly outdid our trade in trinkets. Buoyed by the success of the shop opened beside the arcade, several more had sprung up. It was now difficult for tourists to miss all of them, so by the time they reached the beach, they had already bought anything they needed. Even lowering our prices had not helped us any. All that had done was make people realise they should have waited to buy their stuff until they reached us, but it did not encourage them to buy something again.

"Are we going to have to close?" I asked.

"No. At least, not yet. I don't know." She rubbed at her eyes tiredly. "We need something new, Ro. A gimmick. Something to draw in the customers. Something to set us apart from every other shop just like ours."

I thought hard. I had often given the matter a great deal of consideration, yet had never been able to come up with anything. "How about we clear out anything that doesn't sell?" I asked. "We could build up what does."

"That's just it: none of it sells well any more."

"Beach-balls and towels. T-shirts. We could talk to the suppliers, get a whole new and exclusive range of beach shirts made up."

She managed a tired smile. "I appreciate the enthusiasm, Ro, but I don't think it would work. If business doesn't pick up by the end of summer, we could go under. That gives us some time to play with."

"There must be something we can do."

"Advertising solves most problems, but we tried that and it didn't work, either."

"Advertising? Why don't you stand out on the promenade, reciting Shakespeare?"

At this Jasmine actually laughed. "That's not going to get people flocking to buy towels."

"It might. You'd draw them in, I'm sure."

"You're sweet, but no. My acting days are long behind me, if they ever truly began."

When she was younger, Jasmine had been involved in amateur dramatics. I had never seen her perform, but one time, after I had badgered her for ages about it, she had shown me an old article in a local newspaper. There had been a picture of her, along with the other actors, and the article mentioned her name specifically. 'Young Chakma delivers a superb performance,' the article had read, 'and her characterisation of Desdemona ranks with Suzanne Cloutier and Maggie Smith. One to watch.'

Why she had given up acting, Jasmine had never said, but I always assumed it was just something she'd moved on from. All she had said one time was that she had grown up, but had not elaborated.

She had occasionally given me short bursts of Shakespeare, Wilde and Marlowe, but only because she found my interest endearing. Her performances were always flawless, but also sad, whether they had meant to be or not.

"We'll think of something," I said. "We have a couple of months to go, don't worry too much."

"You're right about the stock that doesn't sell, Ro." She took another swig of water while she thought. "We could do away with the postcards, I guess. No one buys them any more and it might give us more space for keyrings."

"But the seaside without postcards is like marriage without love, or children without toys, or the sun without a smile."

"And us with postcards is like a shop without money in the till."

"If this is progress, Jas, I don't like it."

"Yeah, I'm with you there." Her eyes clouded then and I turned to see what she was looking at. Cara was strolling towards us, dressed as she had been the night before, minus the jacket. She still wasn't wearing her green sandals, but was carrying a sports bag.

"Hey, Ro," she said.

"Cara, hi."

"What can we get you?" Jasmine asked from where she sat.

Cara didn't take her eyes from me. "I'm after something young, gorgeous and fun, but there's nothing on your shelves."

I stifled a giggle but Jasmine was not impressed at all.

"Ro," Cara said, "what time are you lunching?"

"Oh, I hadn't thought. Jasmine?"

"Go when you like," she said. "But I'd like a word first."

"Ooh," Cara said. "A warning."

"A work discussion," Jasmine said icily. "You understand the concept?"

"Work? Yeah, something I try to do as little of as possible, right? You got me pegged, boss." She remained jovial and I could not understand why Jasmine was being this way with her.

"I'll meet you on the beach, Cara," I said. "I'll just be a moment."

"Take your time. Just remember, whatever she says about me is probably true. But then, if I'm too old for you, what does that make her?" She strolled off with a chuckle and raised her arm to wave without turning around.

"Sorry," I said, flushing with embarrassment. It seemed Cara made me do that a lot. "But you could have been a little nicer to her."

"Ro, that woman's trouble."

"No offence, Jas, but you don't know her."

"Neither do you."

"If you're going to tell me to be careful, I already got all this from Sophie."

"Sophie?"

"*Mermaid.*" We had been there a few times together and I had introduced Jasmine to Sophie, but the two women did not really know one another.

"Oh, right," she said. "Seems Sophie knows what she's talking about. Most bar-workers do."

"I know Cara's older than me, Jasmine, but it's only a few years."

"It's not the age difference that worries me. That parting comment about me? That was uncalled for."

"I know; you're not even gay."

"That's irrelevant. She doesn't know me but she's already decided I'm the enemy."

"Just like you've done with her."

"You're right. But, yes, I'm older than you. And with age comes experience. I've been burned before, Ro. I don't want you going through that."

"I wish people would stop treating me like some sweet innocent child. I'm twenty-two, Jas, and I've had plenty of experience with girls."

"I'm not saying you haven't." She wanted to say more, but knew whatever she said would have been wrong. "Go on, then, Ro. Have fun."

"I'll be careful, Jas, I promise. I know what strangers to Glazton can do. They come and they go and get home with fantastic memories, I get all that. I'm not stupid."

"Never thought you were. Go on, she's waiting for you."

Jasmine may have been my boss, but I loved her like a sister. I spent more time with her than anyone else and we had become close. It was just that Glazton was such a small community that everyone seemed to know my business and have their own opinion of it. The most infuriating thing in my life was not having any privacy.

Walking to the beach, I attempted to mimic the cool swagger Cara had perfected, but I was too excited for that. I was not as nervous as I had been the night before, although I was still confused. I hoped that by the end of the lunch-break I would have been able to talk to Cara properly. Perhaps I would go back to work and tell Jasmine she was right, that we had broken off our relationship before it had even begun, or perhaps we would have arranged another date. At the very least, I still hadn't shown Cara any of the sights for her to shoot.

I located her easily enough. She had found a good spot and had opened her sports bag to set down a couple of beach towels. She had brought food as well, and drinks. I was pleased to note she had not brought any alcohol, so it meant she did not have a problem.

"Hey, Cara," I said as I reached her side. "Mind if I strip off?"

"Do I mind if you strip off? How could I possibly mind?"

Her coy smile was back and I lifted off my shirt and sat on the towel she had set up for me before taking off my shoes and shrugging myself out of my trousers. Cara still wore her T-shirt and shorts, which was an odd thing to do at a beach, but perhaps she was cold or something.

"I never lie on the beach in my clothes," I said, removing my watch also and placing it on the towel beside me. "My lunches are spent maintaining my tan."

"That's a fine bikini, Ro."

I had never been self-conscious about my beachwear, for everyone wore versions of something similar. My bra was thin and made of waterproof material. It was green, which was my favourite colour, and matched the lower half of my two-piece bikini. It was as small as it could be so I could make sure my tan touched as much of my body as possible, and no one ever thought there was anything wrong with doing that.

"I'm insanely curious about something," Cara continued from where she lay on her towel beside me, "but it's a little rude to ask."

"You want to know about my tan lines, I take it?"

"Actually, yeah."

"A lot of women lie on their chests and remove their bra-straps so they can get a good tan on their backs, and I do that sometimes, sure. But that doesn't help with my chest and anything, uh, downstairs."

"And?"

"And .., there are places on the beach no one ever goes to. Away from the hubbub of tourists. There are also a few places hidden by rocks."

"Are you telling me you find a hidden place on the beach and sunbathe in the nude?"

"I'm not the only one."

"Being a native has its perks."

"Please stop calling me a native. It's not nice."

"Sure." Her mind was working through something and I wondered what it was. "Anyway, tuck in, Ro. I didn't know what you liked, so I brought a bit of everything."

Cara laid out the food and it was clear she had been to a supermarket or pound shop and bought whatever was on the shelves. There were biscuits, cakes and all manner of chocolate. It seemed Cara was a woman who liked her chocolate.

"Have you taken many photos today?" I asked.

"Nope. I found some old docks or something, but I couldn't find anything interesting. Snapped off a few dozen, but nothing I can use."

"What are you after, exactly?"

"A taste of the seaside. Something exciting, something fresh, something sexy yet rustic. I want people to look at my photos and say to themselves, 'Hey, that's a great place to live', but at the same time I want them to feel a little sad about it. Do you know what I mean?"

"You're an artist; I'm not supposed to know what you mean."

She found that funny and chewed on a Curly Wurly. "Photography is about emotion, Ro. So long as you're evoking emotion, you've succeeded - it doesn't even matter what emotion it evokes - but you also need to give credit to the photographer. Say, for instance, I take a shot of a woman being beaten in the street with a club. People would be angry at that, yes, but they'd be angry at what's being depicted, not the photo itself. To make the photo stand out you need people in the background reacting in horror, some cheering the man on. You need a dog cocking its leg against a tree, uncaring of all these human concerns, you need a seagull taking advantage of the distraction to swoop down and steal someone's dinner."

"Wow," I said, for she had become so animated it was as though she had forgotten I was there with her. "I've never thought of a photograph like that before."

"You're not supposed to. If I do my job right, you'll see all these things in the photo without even noticing them."

I nibbled thoughtfully on a bourbon. "I don't know whether I can find anything like that for you in Glazton. We're a pretty run-of-the-mill place. We're not small, but we're not exactly big, either. There's trouble sometimes, but we're not Blackpool."

"Well, I need something fast. I sent everything I had to one of my publishers this morning and they rejected the whole lot. That's on top of the rejection I got yesterday from another of my publishers."

I figured that was why she had been late for our date. It also went some way to explain her mood. She must have been panicking over her work but trying her hardest to enjoy herself. "Then I need to find you something to take photos of," I said.

"That'd be a godsend. If I don't get some decent material by the end of the day, I'm going to have to pack up and leave."

"Leave?"

"It's not ideal, but it looks like I was wrong. No one wanted the seaside assignments and I figured they were weird for not taking them, but they're more difficult than I imagined. I felt for sure I could just snap pictures of the sea and the beach and I'd be making a fortune. Seems everyone and their granny can do that."

I thought of the postcards which were failing to sell back at the shop. "There must be something I can do," I said. The thought of Cara walking out of my life in search of work elsewhere filled me with dread. We could talk from a distance, so long as Cara would ever give me her number, but it would hardly be the same.

"I'd love for you to help," she said. "I'm just not sure how."

"We could start under the pier. Then we have an old railway, it's been abandoned for years but there's the carcass of a train sitting there. We have a really deep well tourists love to visit, and we have some gorgeous rocks out in the bay."

"The train sounds interesting, but it doesn't scream seaside at me. The well doesn't either; and the pier and rocks are things you can find anywhere. I'm sure they're spectacular and everything, but it needs to be special."

I was struggling for ideas, for the truth was there simply was not much else in Glazton. "The bright lights, then," I said. "The arcades."

"Everywhere has arcades."

"I must be able to do something." I did not mean to wail, but knew I had done so, for people were looking at me. I bit my lower lip and forced myself to breathe steadily until everyone went back to whatever they had been doing.

"You can take my mind off things," Cara said. "I'm so tense, it's a wonder I can think straight at all."

"Yes, yes, I can do that. Whatever I can do to take your mind off your problems, I can do. have you applied suntan lotion today? I could do that for you, it'd be like a massage. Massages relieve tension, right?"

"Are we on a date?"

"I ... Are we?"

"It's just you're offering to massage me and I don't think we've quite got to that stage yet."

"With suntan lotion," I said, throwing a digestive at her. "You should always wear protection on the beach."

"That should so be Glazton's slogan. You'd attract a whole different crowd of people."

I laughed, although the image was horrendous. "I have around forty-five minutes until I need to be back at work. Just tell me what I can do in that time to help you forget your worries."

Propped up on her elbow beside me, she offered a little shrug and leaned towards me. It was an unexpected move and I was not ready for it. Her lips brushed mine, tentatively, and she pulled away with raised eyebrows. I did not need a second invitation and shifted my body into a more comfortable position as I cupped her face with my hand and pressed my lips to hers. She tasted of heat and sweat, but mostly of chocolate. My heart raced, I was fully aware I was dressed only in my two-piece bikini and that there were other people on the beach nearby, but I did not care. I was lying beside a beautiful woman and at last she had instigated the embrace my body had craved for so long.

She placed her hand upon my side as she drew me closer to her and we pressed our bodies together. She was taut beside me, I could feel the tension in her neck as my hand lingered, and she was unable to relax. Closing my eyes, I drifted off into bliss as we embraced, her kisses lingering and leaving me all but panting for more.

We lay beside one another for several minutes, our souls joined as our lips explored the height of simple passion. Finally, Cara pulled away and I gasped, my breath catching in my throat at how happy I was and at how I longed for more.

"Hmm," she mused where she lay. "That certainly took my mind off my problems."

"Glad to be of help," I said, her taste still upon my tongue.

Cara playfully touched my nose with her finger and said, "You, Rowena Shelby, are a bad influence on me. If I stay here much longer, I'll never get any work done."

A sinking feeling tore through my stomach as I glanced at my watch and realised I should have been back at work ten minutes earlier. I was sure we had only been kissing for five minutes, but it had lasted the better part of an hour.

"Jasmine's gonna kill me," I said as I bolted to a sitting position and struggled to get my trousers on.

"Jasmine needs to lighten up," Cara said with a sigh as she lay back down and placed her hands behind her head.

As much as I wanted to stay with Cara, to spend the entire afternoon locked in her embrace, I was distraught at having let Jasmine down. I could imagine her waiting for me, arms folded while she tapped her foot. "Can I meet you tonight?" I asked as I threw my T-shirt over my head and fought to get my arms through. "I can show you something, I've no idea what."

"Sure, hon. You know what, I've just thought of something."

"Something you can shoot?"

"Yeah. Look, Ro, I'm going to be honest with you, Glazton's a bust. Like I said, if I don't get some decent photos by tonight, I'm going to be gone by the morning."

My mind was still frantically on Jasmine, but I could not just leave Cara when she was talking that way. "Then whatever it is you've thought of, I'll take you there."

"It's not quite a place."

"Sorry, Cara, but I'm really late. Could you just tell me what you want me to do?"

"I need to show the glamorous side of Glazton. They won't be used, I just need to show my various bosses that there's worth in this place and that I can get them the goods they want, so long as they give me a little more time."

"Cara, please, just come out with it."

"Would you model for me?"

"Model for you?"

"Yeah, holding a beach-ball and smiling. Maybe in swimwear, I don't know. Glamour shots are where the attention is and if I can show them I can get glamour shots here, they'll give me an extension of at least a few days, maybe even a week."

"A week? That sounds good."

"And they wouldn't use any of the shots, I promise. They'd be promotional pieces, like for my portfolio. They wouldn't be allowed to use the photos unless I sold them to them."

"Cara," I said, placing my hand to her cheek again, "you don't have to explain yourself. Of course I'll do them."

She visibly brightened and at last began to relax. "You will? You're fantastic, Ro."

I kissed her again, but it was rushed. "Sorry, I really have to go. Where shall we meet?"

"My studio. Do you know Taylor Street?"

"Round the back of the cinema?"

"That's the place. Building seven, ask for me by name. They all know me there."

"Building seven, got ya." I needed to run, but I also burned for her so leaned in for a final kiss. She pulled away before I could reach her.

"Ro, you have to get back to work. Hurry."

She was right, but I did not like to leave her when I was so happy. Gathering up anything I had not managed to put back on, I fled across the beach. Jasmine would be angry, but she probably wouldn't say anything. Her angry silences were the worst, but that afternoon I would not mind. Her angry silences would only enable me to fantasise more clearly about this crazy woman with whom I was beginning to think I was falling in love.

# CHAPTER FIVE

Taylor Street was in a rundown area of Glazton. Tucked away at the back of the old cinema, it was a cheap area for rentals and displayed none of the glitz and glamour of the seafront. The buildings were old and grey, tall and thin, and I felt cold wandering around looking for the right address, even though I was wearing long trousers and a jacket. Nights at the seaside did get cold, it's something a lot of people failed to realise, especially the farther one went into town.

I eventually found building seven – the number had fallen off – and saw it was much as the others: a tall building stretching seven or eight storeys with little girth. The door was open so I walked tentatively in. I found myself in a hallway with a couple of doors and a staircase which looked dangerous to walk upon. Not knowing which floor Cara was renting, I started up the stairs, which creaked under my every step.

It was as I reached the second floor that I heard someone talking and saw there was a man through one of the doors.

"Excuse me," I said, "but do you know where Cara is?"

"Cara?" he asked. "The spiky-haired photo girl? Fourth floor."

"Thanks."

Safe in the knowledge that I had the right building, I reached the fourth floor and found two doors, much the same as the other floors. One of the doors was closed, but the other was open and it was to this that I wandered. Peering through, I saw it led to a poky, messy room. The window was formed of thin glass with a single crack down the centre and did nothing to block out the noise of the traffic outside. There was a chest of drawers which had signs of woodworm, and floorboards which had at least two dangerous holes in them. There was no bed in the room, but there was a table over which were strewn photos and notes. A large screen of pinkish brown was set against one wall, with a white board folded three times on hinges so it could stand freely.

Amidst all the madness was Cara Hughes, working frantically to get her cameras onto tripods.

"Cara?"

Her face lit up as she saw me. "Ro. Come on in."

I looked around with barely disguised disgust. Even the ceiling was flaking. "This is where you live?"

"This is where I work. And live, yes. But it's only for a short while, just while I'm in Glazton."

"There's not even a bed."

"I don't really need one. I sleep wherever I fall over."

"And there's no lock on the door."

"No. But my equipment's so antiquated, no one in their right mind would bother touching it."

"You're not *that* old."

"Funny. Sorry to be a pain, Ro, but I'm in a rush. Could you get changed behind the white screen?"

# The Captain's Bombshell

"Sure."

Leaving Cara to her work, I stepped behind the screen. I found a small stool, upon which was folded a blue garment, with a white captain's cap sitting atop. The cap had a blue visor, with a gold tassel and a symbol on the front, probably denoting rank. I tried it on and found it fit snugly while still allowing my red hair to flow either side. It was a prop, that much I could see, but it was symbolic more than anything. No one would think I was a real ship's captain, but it certainly implied something to do with the sea, if not the beach.

Turning my attention to the blue garment, I picked it up with both hands and let it drop. It was a deep-blue single-piece bathing costume with white rimming. It was designed to tightly hug a woman's body and accentuate her curves. A white strap would rise from the cleavage end of the garment and tie it about my neck.

"Uh, Cara?" I called. "This costume's a big raunchy, isn't it?"

"Are you kidding? It's not as revealing as that two-piece bikini you wear on the beach."

Deciding to give it a try, I slipped out of my clothes, thankful for the screen protecting me from Cara. We had only shared our first kiss that afternoon and I was not ready to stand naked before her. Stepping into the garment, I found it even tighter than I had imagined and struggled to tie the white lace about my neck, for the garment hugged me so severely. Eventually, I managed it without help and placed the captain's cap on my head. There was no mirror for me to check myself out, but I twisted and turned as I tried to see myself from every angle.

The garment put an extreme amount of pressure on my breasts and my belly felt as though I was wearing a corset. Nor did the garment go below my hips, and exposed the lower half of my backside. From what I could see from my difficult angle, they hugged my bum cheeks so tightly it was as though the material had been painted on.

I had not felt that uncomfortable in a long time.

"You set, Ro?"

"I'm not sure."

"Come on, step out. Let me take a look at you."

I stepped out, placing the captain's cap back on my head. Cara placed her hands on her hips and looked me up and down appreciatively.

"That," she said, "is the most amazing sight I have ever laid eyes on."

"I don't know," I said, picking at the costume in an attempt to gain some slack. "It's not exactly what I'm used to."

"It's just for a shoot, hon."

"Does it have to be so tight?"

"It might not work for the beach, but these are pretend shots, right? My employers need to see an image of the beach, which isn't necessarily the truth of the beach. What do you know of London?"

"Not much, I've never been there."

"So what do you think you know?"

I thought of my friends who had moved there. "It's grey, there's smog in the air and the pigeons steal food from your hands."

Cara laughed. "I'll admit it's a little grey, but there's no smog and the pigeons aren't seagulls. But if I was to show an image of London to someone who wasn't familiar with it? I'd shoot something grey, smoggy and with pigeons. Maybe not with the pigeons stealing stuff, but I'd certainly cater to the audience if that's what you genuinely think."

"I'm just not sure I'm comfortable wearing this, Cara. I'm taking it off."

Her face fell. "But I don't have anything else for you to wear. Did you bring your bikini?"

"No."

"Then what am I supposed to put you in?"

"I could run home and get it."

"No, no, I need to do this shoot now. I need to fire off the pictures in an e-mail in about two hours. That's just enough time to do the shoot, draft an e-mail and do all the technical stuff with the pictures like processing them. I don't have time for you to run home for a costume even more revealing than this one."

"It's not that it's revealing, Cara. It's just really tight."

"It's supposed to be tight." She placed both hands to her head and ran her fingers through her spiky black hair as she paced. I could tell she was frustrated, perhaps even a little annoyed. "Ro, you said you'd help me. This is my last chance; *you're* my last chance."

"Maybe we could do something else."

"Ro, I can't believe you're … you were my last chance, I have nothing to fall back on. If you weren't going to help me, fine, but you could at least have told me. I've wasted all afternoon setting this up when I could have been out finding something else to shoot."

"I'm sorry, Cara. I'm just not comfortable with posing in this."

"I know, you keep saying." She continued to pace and I could see in her eyes that she was silently firing off possibilities and just as quickly discarding them. "I don't know what I'm going to do."

"I feel terrible."

"Bully for you."

I did feel terrible and desperately wanted to suggest some alternative, but I had already done that and Cara had not liked any of them. The railway, the pier, the amazing well ... she could have been out shooting one of those and would at least have had something to work with. Instead, I'd ruined everything. I could potentially have destroyed her career. If she had never wandered into my shop to buy some sandals, she would have managed to get what she needed for work.

"I'll do it," I said, my voice cracking because I really didn't want to.

"No, no, if you're not comfortable, I'm not going to force you." She had yet to stop pacing. "I need something quick, I need something now. I just honestly have no idea how I'm coming back from this."

"Cara, I'll do it. The photos aren't going to be sold, right? They're just going in your portfolio, so you can stay here another few days?"

"Yeah."

"Then I'll do it. I'm not going to ruin your life, Cara, and if helping you out like this keeps you in my life a little longer, I have absolutely no problem with that."

"Hon, are you sure?"

I took a deep breath, which was a little difficult in that get-up. "Yes."

"Oh, Ro, you're the best." She stopped pacing and grinned. Hastening over to her various cameras, she selected one she had set up on a tripod. "Stand in front of that wall, if you don't mind. The pinky-brown one."

I did as instructed and for the next twenty minutes or so Cara photographed me. She must have taken a hundred shots or more, in various poses, from various angles. She had a beach-ball for me to play with, a bucket and spade to hold, she even had me apply suntan lotion to my skin and took rather a lot of shots of this process.

"All right," she said at last. "Just a few more and we're done."

"Gosh, I never knew modelling could be so exhausting."

"I'd offer you a break, but my deadline's battering me in the face."

I did not complain and stood as directed. Cara wanted me to stand with my legs to the side, almost facing the wall, with my torso twisted so I was facing the camera. The angle put a tremendous strain on my costume and I could feel the material clinging painfully to my bum cheeks which were, of course, facing the camera. I noticed Cara had opted to use a handheld camera for these shots and was alternately crouching and standing to get the optimum positions.

"OK," she said, "drop your right arm and tilt your wrist so your fingers are lightly brushing your thigh. Keep your arm straight but a little lower. I need to get your right breast in shot."

I glanced surreptitiously at my chest but the costume was still in place. She had meant she needed my breast to be seen by the camera, with the costume over the top.

"Perfect," she said. "Now, your left arm, bend it and keep the elbow to your side. I don't want it in the shot. Your fingers need to be by your chin, playing with that amazing red hair of yours. Raise a finger if you can ... Excellent. The cap's in the right place, your hair's bouncing all by itself – oh, you're wonderful, Rowena. Your lips. Stop smiling."

"Stop smiling?"

"I need you coy, almost pouty. I'm going for sexy here, not happy. I need to see those full red lips. And your eyes, make them wider. Let me see those gorgeous green wonders of yours."

She merrily snapped off at least fifty more photos. It was difficult, actually quite painful, keeping that pose, but I would do it for Cara. At last, she announced we were done and I was able to relax.

"I need to get this thing off," I said, not quite having expected to be sweating so much.

"Actually, that's something I wanted to talk to you about."

"Hmm?"

"I'll be honest, Ro, I'm massively excited right now. I have enough material here to save my career.

Anyone looking at these shots will take me seriously. I'll probably be able to stay at least a couple more months now, right up until the weather starts getting cold."

I was thrilled by the news and had never seen her so elated.

"How would you feel if I took a few for myself?" she asked.

"Sure. Keep whatever you want of them."

"I meant something else. I don't work with models too often but you're the best I've ever known. I'd really love a few topless photos, though."

I blinked. "Excuse me?"

"All models do it sooner or later."

"I'm not a model."

"I know, you're my girlfriend."

My heart skipped a beat at that. Things had been going so slowly between us and now they were moving incredibly quickly. I could not keep up with what was going on.

"They wouldn't go in my portfolio, obviously," she said. "I just figured while we're here, we could get serious with our relationship. And since I'm a photographer, getting serious for me is taking a few topless shots."

"I don't know. I ..."

"It's cool if you don't want to do it. But you have that picture of the two of us from the booth. Only seems fair I get a few of you in return."

"You already have a lot of me in return."

"Nah, those are for my portfolio. I meant for me. Something private, something no one else will see. Something to remind me how fabulous my girlfriend is when I'm really depressed about how much work I have to do."

I licked dry lips, fighting to reach an answer. The costume was so restricting, the shoot so long that I was feeling light-headed. I wanted to please Cara, I wanted to keep her, and if she was prepared to consider us girlfriends, I did not want to upset her and chase her away. We had such potential together, we were just starting out on our relationship, that I did not want to ruin it by being childish. I was still agonisingly aware that I was younger than Cara and wanted to avoid her even thinking about it. She said she had worked with models before, she had said it was something all models did eventually, and if she could start seeing me as a model, it would mean she would want to keep me in her life forever.

"All right," I said. "But just a few."

"Great, Ro. OK, undo the white lace around your neck. Good, good. Now, peel the top down slightly. Slowly, slowly," she said as she snapped off a dozen shots a second. "Keep going, but slowly."

Using both hands, I peeled down my top. It was exciting, yet at the same time unnerving. I had been naked with women before, of course, but this was something different. Revealing my breasts to Cara in that fashion stirred something within me, for it was certainly the kinkiest thing I had ever got up to. Forcing myself to relax, I drew the top down until my breasts were almost fully exposed. Cara continued snapping away all the while. At last, I had drawn my top down to the base of my breastbone, revealing my chest in its entirety. It was strange to be exposing myself to this woman I had only so recently met, but I no longer felt quite so uncomfortable. I was glad I had my all-over tan, for it would make the pictures so much better.

"Pout, Ro. Good. Lower lip out a bit more ... fantastic. Cup your breasts. Great stuff. Could you pinch a nipple?"

"No."

"No? Really?" She looked at me with a hurt expression.

I reconsidered and pinched a nipple. Over the next five minutes, I did a few other things with which I was not entirely comfortable, and by the end I was dripping with sweat.

"Fantastic," Cara said. "Could you drop the bathing costume a little more? It's getting in the way of my shots."

I struggled it a little lower so it exposed my belly. It clung to my hips, which was a little strange considering it did not travel much past them. Cara continued taking photos and had stopped talking to me. I was beginning to lose my excitement.

"I think that's enough," I said.

"A little more. It's just one more step, you know. Go on, chuck the costume, but leave the hat."

"No."

"Ro, you're practically naked. It's just one more step."

"I don't want you to have nude photos of me."

She looked at me from over her camera, hurt in her eyes. "Seriously? You're not going full nude?"

"Of course I'm not going full nude. Cara, we only kissed this afternoon."

"This isn't a sexual thing, Ro, it's work. This is how I express myself, and it's how my girlfriend should express herself."

"There's a difference between expressing and exposing."

"Exposure's just another term for a photographer." She narrowed an eye. "All right, if you're not going to do it, you're not going to do it."

"I'm not going to do it."

"Fine. You might as well go behind the screen and get changed. Behind the screen, where you don't want me seeing you."

"Cara, don't be like that."

"Please don't do that. Just get changed while I sort out my cameras."

I felt bad as I changed, although a part of me was angry, because I shouldn't have felt bad at all. It was my body and if I didn't want to bear it all for Cara, then I didn't have to. She wasn't paying me, I didn't work for her. We were supposed to be girlfriends and she was treating me like a tool.

By the time I was back in my own clothes, Cara's mood had shifted back to glee. "I'm sorry, Ro," she said. "I shouldn't push you into doing something you don't want to. I just get so intense when I'm working. When something I'm shooting doesn't behave the way I want it to, I get frustrated. I sometimes forget when I'm shooting people and that people have feelings."

"It's all right. Can I help with the cameras?"

"No, I'm good, thanks. If you don't have experience with them, you could end up wiping something."

"Oh. OK. Anything I can do at all?"

"Uh, no."

"I can hang around? Offer moral support."

"No, no, I'm good. Look, Ro, not to be annoying, but I have that deadline. Please, I need to be alone to get my work done."

"Oh. OK."

"But I'll call you, all right? You'll be hearing from me so soon, you'll think I'd left here with you."

I smiled, she returned the smile and I moved in for another kiss.

"Deadlines, Ro. There'll be more than enough time for that sort of thing later. Once I have my work accepted, once I have some money, we'll take time to relax. With photos like these, I'll probably be here all summer. You can show me the real sights of Glazton, we can spend all day kissing on the beach, and maybe I can even get to see you naked, but without the cameras." She winked and I grinned broadly.

"I wouldn't want to get in your way," I said. "Talk to you soon, then."

"Thanks, Ro. I mean that. Thanks for everything."

I skipped merrily from her studio and made my way back to the street. Breathing deeply of the clean sea air, I said good evening to the gulls eating out of a torn bin-liner. It was not until I got home that I realised one very annoying thing.

Cara was going to call me, but I still didn't have her number. I considered going back to her, but I would only be in the way. She would probably pop by the shop in the morning and tell me how everything with her portfolio went. Yes, I would see her in the morning. In the meantime, I needed some sleep. I was exhausted.

# CHAPTER SIX

I didn't hear anything for a week and my life continued in a daze. I did not know what to do, for I did not want to bother Cara. She was obviously very busy with her work and if her portfolio was satisfactory to her various employers, there was every chance she had gained her extension. She had said if all went well, she would be able to stay a couple of months and if I blundered back into her studio, I might set her back. She had been delayed, that was all, and since she had entirely forgotten to give me her number, she could not contact me to let me know she had to concentrate on her work.

My father had asked me a few times how I was getting on with Cara but I was always vague and tended to go up to my room whenever he brought her up. My sister pestered me for the first few days, always after juicy gossip, but I overheard my father telling her to leave me alone and she had not bothered me since. He was not angry about it, but concerned, and I spent every night lying in my bed with my face in my pillow, trying not to cry loudly enough to let any of them overhear.

At work, Jasmine was good enough not to mention Cara at all, although I could tell she wanted to. Jasmine had wanted Cara kept away from my workplace and that was precisely what she was doing, so Jasmine had no reason to complain. She was worried about me, but I knew she would not say anything at all unless I brought the matter up myself, and I had no intention of doing that.

Behind the counter, I would often glance out to the promenade in case Cara was coming by, and my lunch-times were spent as ever on the beach. For the past week, I had spent them in the same spot, that magical place where Cara and I had kissed, in the hope she would return.

After a week of all of this repeating itself over and over, I began to suspect something had happened. Perhaps Cara had been called away from Glazton by one of her employers who needed to meet her in person; or perhaps the bailiffs had caught up to her; or maybe she had been in an accident. I ran a lot of scenarios through my head during that week, for Cara occupied my every waking thought and most of my slumbering ones. I would give her one more day, I promised myself: one more day before I went to the studio to talk with her. It was always just one more day I would give her.

The one possibility which I refused to entertain was also the likeliest – it was the one Jasmine, my father and even my sister would have said was most plausible if I had taken any of them into my confidence. There was a chance Cara just no longer wanted to talk to me, did not want to see me any more. Maybe I was a bad kisser, maybe she had already found someone else – maybe she was even with someone else already and I was nothing more than a holiday fling for her. I tried to work out what I had done wrong, and it all boiled down to the studio. I had posed for her, I had posed a lot more than I had intended, but I had insulted her profession when I had refused to go full nude. Nudity was not something artists saw as obscene, for they had been painting nudes for centuries. By refusing to take the swimsuit completely off, I was effectively belittling her profession. I was like an art critic who condemned something as disgusting without understanding the true nature of art.

There was a chance Cara hated me because I could not fully understand her work. She could not have a girlfriend who treated her that way, so she had stopped seeing me entirely.

Of course, I did not know the truth, and that was the worst part of it all.

I was in the shop when something happened to spur me into action. I was serving a customer, a man in his twenties. He was buying a couple of postcards – we still had not made a decision on whether to stop selling them – when he frowned.

"Don't I know you from somewhere?" he asked.

I tried not to roll my eyes but knew I had not succeeded. "Does that line ever work?" I asked, for I had already ruined my standard smile-and-decline routine.

"No, no, I'm serious," he said, rubbing his chin in thought. I had never actually seen someone rub their chin in thought so knew it must be serious.

"Sorry," I said, "but if we've met, I don't remember you."

"It's the hair," he said, musing, but not in a creepy way; nor was he trying to chat me up. It threw me a little because it felt as though he was not after anything. We were of a similar age, so I said, "Maybe we went to school together."

"Maybe. Did you have your hair like that back then?"

"Uh, sometimes." I pouted while I tried to remember, and recognition flashed in his eyes as he snapped his fingers.

"Now I know. The pout gave it away. Ha! Captain's Bombshell."

"Is that a club?"

"Is that a club, she says. Oh, you crack me up. What are you doing working here?"

"I always work here. It pays the rent."

"It pays the rent, she says. You're something else, Captain." He took a step back, saluted me and went off with his postcards. It was a truly odd experience and one which left me with a sinking pit in my stomach. There had been something in his eyes after he had recognised me, something almost leering.

The man's attitude bugged me for the next hour and made me anxious every time I had to serve a customer. I smiled all the while, refusing to go anywhere near a pout, and when Jasmine came by at last, I asked whether I could take a break.

"Sure," she said. "Something wrong?"

"No. I just need to check something. Can I use the computer?"

"Yeah."

We had a laptop for work purposes. Jasmine had bought it cheaply and kept it in a little locked cabinet under the counter, along with any valuables either of us had which we did not want to keep on our persons. She unlocked the cabinet and passed the laptop over to me without a word. It was not supposed to be used for non-work purposes, but Jasmine did not mind if I searched the Internet during stormy weather. I had to spend my lunch-breaks doing something, and even I didn't lie on the beach when it was raining.

Not wanting to take the laptop away from the shop (and probably not being allowed to anyway) I sat on a box behind the counter and started it up while Jasmine took over duties on the till. It took a while to boot up, mainly because Jasmine had bought it *really* cheaply, although once it had done so I tentatively opened the Internet browser and brought up a search engine. It was only as I was typing 'Captain's Bombshell' that I realised I was pouting and immediately plastered a fake smile to my face.

"Ro?" Jasmine asked. "You're not looking up anything dodgy on my laptop, are you? Only, your face just went all shades of weird."

"I hope not."

"That's not reassuring."

I looked to the screen. There were not a lot of results – mainly it offered me the definition of both words – so I hit the button to search for images.

My face fell, I struggled for breath and heard the wheeze catch in my throat as I almost dropped the machine.

"Ro? Ro, are you all right?"

I blinked, blinked again, stared at Jasmine and tried to say something, but instead I rasped heavily. She tried to see the screen of the laptop and I fumbled to close it, although my hands would not obey my brain.

A customer asked a question about paying by credit card and Jasmine turned from me to deal with her. It afforded me precious seconds to look back to the laptop. There, emblazoned on the screen before me, was the image of a young woman standing before a pinkish-brown background. She was half-facing the wall so her bum was pointed at the camera – a bum which was tightly wrapped in a one-piece blue swimming costume. The fingers of her right hand were brushing the skin of her thigh, the fingers of her left were playing with her bouncing red hair, while a blue costume-covered breast peered out from where her body was turning to the camera. Her expression was pouty and her green eyes shone eerily through from the expert camerawork. Upon her head was a white captain's cap, with a blue visor and gold lace.

It was one of the many pictures Cara had snapped of me.

Underneath the picture were the words 'The Captain's Bombshell'.

"Ro, are you all right?"

I quickly hit the X in the corner and the image vanished. "Fine," I said, looking at her, my heart having stopped some moments earlier. "Never better. I'm done."

"You sure you don't want to delete your Internet history first?"

I handed the laptop over, then snatched it back as my heart thumped painfully after so long of inaction. "I'd better turn it off," I said. "Don't want to waste the battery." Without waiting for a reply, I re-opened the Internet and delete the history before turning the whole thing off.

Jasmine was staring at me when I was finished. "Ro, you're scaring me."

"I'm fine."

"You're not fine."

"I'm not fine. But I'm going to be fine. I'm ..." I had no idea how I was going to be fine. Cara had promised not to sell those pictures, that they had just been for her portfolio, yet there they were all over the Internet. That must have been where that customer had seen the images, but why would Cara have lied to me? Was she offered so much money for them that she felt she had to sell them? Did the bailiffs demand them? Was that why she had not come to see me since – because she was embarrassed or ashamed?

How could she have sold them? How could she have betrayed me like that? How was I going to explain it to Jasmine if she ever found out? How was I going to explain it to my father? He was so understanding about me, had never once called me weird or odd because of my sexuality. He said he loved me and always would love me for who I was; but how could I possibly explain that I had posed in a swimming costume like some pin-up girl?

I choked as something else occurred to me. Those had not been the only photographs Cara had taken. She had promised the topless ones would be just for her, yet she had also promised she would never sell the swimsuit ones. If she had gone back on her word about the costumed ones, there was every chance she had also sold ...

My body shook uncontrollably and I lurched forward. I just managed to get my head outside the shop before I vomited. Two passers-by looked at me oddly as they continued walking and in their eyes all I could see were accusations. 'Strumpet,' they were saying. 'Filthy whore.'

I looked to the beach to see a father and mother tossing a disc around with their son. They were far away but I knew they were looking at me. 'Stay away from my family,' they were saying. 'You should be ashamed.'

On top of the shop, a seagull laughed at my foolishness, its eyes manic as it said, 'Got what you deserved, you dirty little tramp.'

"Ro!"

"Wha ...?"

"Rowena, can you hear me?"

I turned to find Jasmine was holding onto me, for I had all but fallen out of the shop. She helped me back to the box and told me to sit with my head between my knees and take deep breaths. After a few of those, she raised my head and I felt my lips moisten as she tipped water into my mouth from a bottle.

"Small sips," she said. "There, are you OK?"

"No. Yes. Oh my God." My head fell into my hands and I wept shuddering tears.

"Ro," she said, crouching before me and taking me by the shoulders. "Ro, you need to tell me what's wrong and you need to tell me right now."

I moved my hands from my eyes and looked at her. She was worried and terrified and I opened my mouth to tell her everything, but I couldn't say a word. I was so ashamed by what I had done, by what Cara had done to me, and I couldn't even speak.

All I could think of was how much it would hurt my father when he found out his little girl was nothing more than a porn-site sex worker.

But no, I did not know anything for sure. All I knew was that one photo – a single photo – that Cara had taken had managed to get onto the Internet with the headline 'The Captain's Bombshell'. Beyond that, everything was speculation. I needed to confront Cara, I needed to find out the truth. If she had made a mistake, I needed her to admit it to my face so we could hopefully sort the matter out once and for all. The photograph had been stolen, that was all. Someone had stolen it from her and she had spent all week trying to get it back. Once she found out I knew, everything would be all right, because we could tackle the problem together.

I stood so suddenly the blood rushed to my head and I almost collapsed.

"I need to go," I said.

"You need to go home and lie down," Jasmine said. "But you're not in a fit state to do that by yourself. Give me a minute to close up the shop and I'll walk you home."

"No. You can't lose trade."

"You're more important, Ro."

"I'm fine."

"You keep saying that but we both know it's not true. I'm calling your father."

"No," I said in horror. "Jasmine, you can't call my father like I'm some misbehaving teen. I'm twenty-two, I'm not a child."

"It's not about being a child. You have a family who love you and one of them needs to come fetch you. I'm not letting you walk home by yourself."

"It's a short walk and the sea air will do me good."

"Ro, listen."

"I know you mean well, but I don't have to listen. If you're sending me home, I'll go home. But I can get there by myself."

"I don't like this."

"You don't have to. I'll call you when I get home."

"Make sure you do. If I haven't heard from you in an hour, I'm calling your dad, and I don't care how old you are."

An hour. It would be enough time to get to the studio and then back home, but only if I hurried. "Great. Thanks, Jas, you're the best boss ever."

I ran without waiting for her to reply. I ran and did not stop running until I arrived, breathless and giddy, outside the studio. Taking a moment to steady myself, I fought the nausea rising through my body, for I did not want to vomit on Cara's doorstep. Taking a few deep breaths of the sea air did indeed steady my body, if not my nerves, and I was at last ready to face the woman who had unwittingly caused me so much anguish.

The front door was once again open and I hastened up to the fourth floor. The doors to the two rooms on that floor were both open and I rushed into Cara's studio, and stopped. Her equipment was gone, her notes were gone. The white screen was still there, as was the pinkish-brown backdrop before which I had stood to pose. Of Cara's effects there was no sign at all.

"You all right there, miss?"

I spun to find a man coming out the other door. I could see in his own room he had canvases set up, with paint all over the floor and down his clothes. My brain told me he was a painter, that he had rented his studio to get some work done, but I did not care for any of that.

"Cara," I said. "Where's Cara?"

"Cara's gone, miss. You want maybe to sit down? You don't look so good."

"Gone?"

"Moved on. Went back to wherever she came from, probably. I didn't know her too well but I think she came from London."

"She can't be gone."

"Well, she's not here. These places are rentals. Her lease probably ran out so she left."

"She must have set herself up somewhere else."

"I doubt it. This is the cheapest place in town for studios. It's why we're all here."

Panic rose through me but I fought it down with reason. "If this place is so cheap, someone must be moving in."

"That's right, yes. I reckon someone will."

"So Cara must have moved out this morning."

"I get caught up in my work, sorry. I didn't notice. I haven't seen her around in a couple of days, though."

"This can't be happening." I perched on Cara's table before I fell. My body was trembling and I held a hand to my face as my tears attempted to flow, but crying would not help me.

"You really don't sound good," the man said. "Here, let me get you some water. I have something stronger if you want it."

"I don't drink," I snapped. "Why can't people just accept that?"

"Only trying to help."

I felt bad for shouting at him but I had more pressing concerns. "Sorry," I said. "Do you know what Cara does for a living?"

"Photography, yes."

"Have you heard of the Captain's Bombshell?" I asked tremulously, fearful she had been displaying my image all over the building.

"No," he said. "Is that a nightclub?"

I laughed at the absurdity of the both of us thinking the same thing. "Something like that. Did you ever see any of her pictures?"

"No. Well, a few. There were pictures of seagulls but they weren't very good. And buildings. Old buildings, but they didn't impress me, either. Proper lighting, that's what she needed. And you only get proper lighting in a studio, where you can control everything. Photography is all about control, miss. Light, distance, pose ... so long as you have complete control over your subject, you can get some great shots." He paused. "I used to do some photography myself but I concentrate on painting now. Did I say something wrong?"

I reacted badly to his words. I knew I was gasping, knew I was about to lose control of my bladder and possibly my bowels and was glad I was perched on the table, for I would have curled into a pathetic ball on the floor. His words stung. Cara needed complete control of her subject, which meant everything she had said to me had been a lie designed to win my trust. She had been using me since the day we had met, had always intended to get nude shots of me and had done everything she needed in order to entrap me.

"Do you ..." I asked, but my throat cracked and I coughed to clear it. "Do you know who she worked for?"

"No. She mentioned a few bits and pieces here and there, but I wasn't really listening."

"Any glamour magazines?"

"Glamour mags? Now that you mention it, she did say she was working on getting a contract for top-shelf magazines. Said she'd sold some freelance to them now and again and was looking to get a steady wage."

It took several moments for his words to sink in. That Cara had posted swimsuit pictures of me in the Internet was bad enough, but my greatest fear had been those topless shots. If Cara had contacts in the porn industry, there could well have been photographs of me spread all over the place.

Bile rose in my throat at what I had done, at how foolish I had been. I had been stupid enough to fall in love with a woman everyone had warned me against and now that woman was destroying my life.

I caught sight of something then, something in the bin by the door. There were cartons of leftover food there, along with dirty tissues, but there was also something else. A familiar bear we had won together from the hook-a-duck: the bear Cara had kept as a memento of our time together. The teddy stared sadly up at me with button eyes which told me the bear had been trying to warn me all along.

I ran from the studio, heedless of the kind man who had tried to help me. I could barely see for tears, could barely hear for the pounding between my ears, and I burst onto the street and ran in front of a car which blared its horn at me. I did not stop, hardly even noticed, and ran all the way home.

My sister would have been at work but my father was in and peered over at me with concern as he worked in the kitchen. "Ro? What happened?"

I did not stop to talk but fled upstairs and hurled myself onto my bed. Sinking my face into my pillow, I wept and wept, screaming into my pillow and hoping it drowned out some of the noise. After a while, my father came up to my room and sat on the bed beside me. He gently caressed my back, which was something which had always calmed me when I was a little girl. But I was no longer a little girl and there was every chance he would soon find out just how much I had grown.

Soon, everyone I knew would find out how much I had grown.

He spent a long time trying to talk with me, but I did not respond. Eventually, he gave up and went back downstairs. He knew I needed my space, knew my problem was something I had to work through myself, and he was good enough to let me deal with it. He knew I would speak with him when I was ready, just as I always did. But this was something I would not talk to him about, ever. This was not like the time I had an ugly break-up with Gloria, nor was it like the time I had got into a fight with Ed because his sister and I had shared a kiss. This was different. This time, I could not make amends.

And I had no one to blame but myself.

# CHAPTER SEVEN

I did not speak much to my family the following morning. My sister had already gone to work so I had breakfast with my father but did not eat a thing. He asked me what was wrong and I have no idea what I said but it was probably a whole lot of nothing. As breakfast wore on, I knew I was going to have a confrontation with my father. I would either continue to say nothing or explode in anger at him, but he was within his rights to demand to know what had me so glum.

Instead, he just sat opposite me over the breakfast table and looked at me with sad eyes. I played my spoon around my cornflakes and refused to meet his gaze. I was ashamed and I hated myself.

"I don't know what's wrong, Ro," he said at last, "and you don't have to tell me. But it's not as bad as you think."

"What if it is?" I asked lamely.

"It's not."

I said nothing.

"I got a call from Jasmine yesterday."

I still said nothing.

"She's worried about you but didn't say much. She wanted to make sure you got home safely."

Jasmine had not told him about the laptop, which was something at least. I had horrible visions of my father opening his Internet browser and seeing images of me pop up all over the place. It would have been kind to tell him, rather than have him find out about me that way, but I could not bring myself to say anything. My father was my hero, he always had been, and he was the most understanding man I had ever known.

"I just want to ask you a couple of things," he said uncomfortably.

I shrugged.

"Whatever's happened ... because something's definitely happened ... whatever's happened, is anyone hurt? Physically hurt? No one's died or anything?"

I shook my head.

"And you. You haven't been ...? I mean, you didn't get attacked by anyone who ...?"

At last I looked up at him and saw the hurt in his eyes. He had spent all night worrying about me and in my selfishness all I had thought about was myself. "No," I said, a shudder shooting through my body. "No, I ... No, I haven't been raped or anything."

His shoulders sagged with relief. "Thank God for that."

Tears misted my eyes at what I had put my father through and I bit my lip. I did not want to tell him I felt as though I *had* been raped, although even saying such a thing would have been disrespectful to genuine victims. I was not a victim, after all, I was an idiot.

"I'm not going to ask anything else, then," he said. "Although, and you don't have to confirm this, but I'm assuming this has to do with Cara."

I nodded slightly: he deserved that much at least.

"And you don't want to talk about it?"

I shook my head.

"Ro," he said, taking a deep breath, "I'm not going to lecture you because you really don't need that. But we've all been where you're at. I don't know what happened, but if you and Cara have split up, maybe it was for the best. Before it got serious between the two of you." He paused. "Did it get serious between the two of you?"

"I didn't sleep with her."

He nodded slowly. I had held such frank discussions with my father before. As I said, he was an understanding man and I was always comfortable talking with him. It did not mean I would rush to him every time I kissed a new girl or did something more than that, but certainly when I was upset I would tell him my problems.

That I was telling him nothing this time must have hurt him more than anything else.

"I'm sorry, Dad," I said.

"I forgive you."

"But you don't even know what I've done."

"Did you hit her?"

"No."

"Did you push her in front of a bus?"

"No."

"Did you hurt her or did she hurt you?"

My voice cracked as I said, "She hurt me."

"Then you don't even need forgiveness."

I continued to look him in the eyes as I tried to get out everything that needed to be said, although I knew I was a coward and that I would never reveal it all.

"Dad, if I did something you wouldn't be proud of …"

"I'd still love you and I'd still protect you."

"What if it was really bad?"

"Then I'd go down to Jasmine, buy a spade off her and bury the body."

I laughed. For a moment, I actually laughed, before the horror of the situation sank back in upon me.

"That's a good sound," he said.

I tried a smile for him, but it was difficult. "I love you, Dad. Please remember that."

"I never doubted it. Why?" I could see he wanted to ask me again what I had done, but was respectful enough not to.

"I want to tell you," I said. "But I can't."

"Will I find out eventually?"

I nodded my head.

"Then I want you to know that when I do, I won't judge you. Whatever you've done, you didn't do it for hateful reasons. You didn't do it because you're a wicked person, you did it because you're kind and caring. Too caring."

"How do you know that?"

"Because I know you, Ro. And you could never harm anyone."

"I'll harm you when this comes out."

"No. You just think you will."

But I did not just think I would, for I knew what I had done and he did not. "I'd better get to work."

"You didn't eat when you came home yesterday and you haven't eaten this morning."

"I wouldn't be able to hold anything in."

"Promise me you'll eat something."

"I promise." I rose and grabbed my bag for work. I was halfway to the door when my father called me back.

"Your lunch," he said, holding out some foil-wrapped sandwiches he had removed from the fridge.

I took the package and slipped it into my bag, knowing I was going to throw it away before I returned home. I did not meet his gaze again because my resolve had already deteriorated. "I love you, Dad," I said again as though it was a sentiment which needed reinforcing.

He hugged me, tightly, and in that hug I could feel his concern. It took me a moment to react, but then I hugged him back. In that moment I almost blurted out everything, but I was strong enough, or weak enough, not to.

I went to work, wandering miserably through the streets of Glazton and wishing the ground would collapse beneath me to swallow my shame whole.

I arrived at work a little late, mainly because I did not want to face Jasmine. She had called my father and I wanted to be angry with her, wanted to shout at her to mind her own damn business and to stop treating me like a child; but I did not. For one thing, that would have been rude, and for another I knew she did nothing through spite. There were so many people in my life who cared about me, it was a shame I has not listened to any of them.

Jasmine said nothing about my being late and I grumbled a good morning as I moved behind the counter. We already had a few customers in the shop, of which I was grateful, for Jasmine would never discuss our private lives while in earshot of customers. She did hang around, however, which told me she had no intention of leaving me alone for the whole day. I resented that, but I was also glad, since I did not know what I would do if someone else should recognise me.

I had been at work for around an hour and in all that time we had spoken only about work. My answers were short, to the point, and Jasmine was kind enough not to pry.

"We're getting a new delivery tomorrow," she said. "I'm trying out a few new items which might keep us afloat."

"OK."

"I want you to clear out some of the old stock. We need to make some room."

"OK."

"The postcards are going to have to go. We decided that already, right? Oh nuts. I forgot to tell the suppliers I didn't want any more postcards. I bet they've put some in."

"We could always send them straight back."

"We'll have to — it's too late to cancel the order now. Anyway, when we have a period that's not very busy, I want you to clear out anything we don't sell. It'll give you something to focus on."

"Thanks."

She quirked a smile. "I may not be asking you what's wrong, Ro, but I'm not an idiot. And right now, having something to occupy your mind is the best thing for you."

I spent the rest of the morning around the shop while Jasmine minded the till. The postcards were the first things to go. We might have been able to get some return on them from the suppliers, so I did not throw them in the bin. The seaside trinkets were something I had to deal with as well, although most of those I was knocking down in price rather than removing entirely. I suspected Jasmine's delivery would consist mainly of beach items, which were in the main quite large, so we needed plenty of hanging space but not necessarily a lot of room on the shelves.

Jasmine was right in that it kept my mind occupied, and by lunch-time I had even managed to get my mind off my problems for a short while.

"Go get something to eat," Jasmine said when I was done.

"I brought sandwiches."

"Then do yourself a favour and eat them."

She was right; but then, Jasmine was my boss so she was paid to be right. Feeling a little better about things, I took my foil-wrapped sandwiches and the rest of my bag down to the beach. I was no longer waiting for Cara so chose a different part of the sand to lie on. Setting down my towel, I stripped off my T-shirt and trousers, as was my routine, and settled down on my back. I would eat, I promised myself, but for a few minutes I just wanted to feel the sun on my skin, like an old friend welcoming me into her arms.

Cara was never far from my mind and I no longer even knew what to think about her. I was conflicted, for on the one hand I hated her for what she had done, yet on the other I was certain there had to have been an explanation. Cara would not have betrayed me, she would have her reasons for doing what she had done. She was not a cruel or vindictive woman, for I had seen a kinder, caring side to her. That could not have been a lie – Cara could not have been a lie. What we shared could not have been a lie.

Love was not a lie, I would not believe it.

I opened my eyes when I realised someone was laughing. Turning my head, I could see two young men and a woman looking at me. One of the men was pointing and I quickly checked my bikini in case in my haste I had not fastened it correctly. I could not understand what they were laughing at.

Then I heard the word.

Bombshell.

Bolting to a sitting position, I tried to shout at them, tried to scream, but nothing emerged. One of the men wolf-whistled and the other man doubled over in hysterics, while the woman was doing both.

All over the beach, people were reacting. A family had stopped tossing around their ball to see what the commotion was, a man in his fifties was coming over angrily to tell the trio to stop accosting me, while two young boys copied the wolf-whistles without the first clue as to what they were doing. All around me, people were whispering, and everyone had an opinion.

It was only from those three that I had heard the word Bombshell, yet it did not matter, for it had been enough.

Clambering to my feet, I grabbed my bag and fled, stumbling after my first step and slamming my knee into the sand. Tears filled my eyes but I did not take the time to even angrily wipe them away as I fled. My bag, half open, spilled its contents everywhere, but I did not stop to gather anything. I simply ran.

My routine was ruined. I could no longer spend my lunch-breaks on the beach. Cara had stolen from me my one simple pleasure in life.

I could not return to the shop so ran to the public toilet standing close to the beach. It was spacious inside, although the floor was wet with so many people having washed themselves down after a dip in the sea. I found an empty cubicle and sealed myself in, locking the door and sitting on the toilet. There I sat and cried for a long time, the pain of life slicing into my very soul.

How so many people had seen those images was beyond me. How so many people could not only have seen them but had also recognised me was not possible. Yet it had happened. The images could not therefore have only been on that one website. It was the magazines Cara worked for. They had nude pictures of me and they had already published them. I had visions of topless images of me being posted in phone booths or plastered over toilet walls along with my mobile number. If I went through town at night, I would see a thousand bulbs flashing in a montage of my striptease.

Finally, I had no more tears to shed and I leaned back where I sat and took deep breaths. My heart was pounding so fiercely I thought it would break. I wished it would. I wished I would die in that cubicle, alone and shamed. I wished for so many things, yet above all I wanted the humiliation to end. And I did not want to be around when my family found out what I had done.

I noticed then my bag was open and remembered I had lost most of my belongings. My towel was still on the beach, my water flask, the book my sister had lent me. Even my sandwiches were gone, no doubt having been devoured by seagulls. My father had made those specially and I had promised to eat them. I could not even get that right.

Standing, I found my legs wobbly, due to lack of food as much as from terror, and opening the door I took up my bag and walked back to the shop. I no longer had my watch, for I had left it on the towel so I would not get a tan line around my wrist, so did not know how late I was. Jasmine was waiting for me and she looked more relieved than I had ever seen her.

"Ro, you're all right."

"Sorry I'm late. If I'm late. I guess I must be late." I noticed my beach towel was behind the counter, along with my sandwiches and watch. In fact, all my things were there, and I was a little confused.

"A kind man brought them over to me," she explained. "He told me there was a group of young people jeering at you and that you ran off crying. He gave them what for. From what I hear, I think he put the fear of God into them."

"How did he know where I worked?"

"You're a regular on the beach. I think a lot of the locals know you work here. He was worried about you. *I'm* worried about you." She paused. "I'm sorry, Ro, I called your father."

"You what?"

"I didn't know where you were. This man who brought all your stuff, he said you'd run off but he didn't see where. You're dressed in a bikini and you're not thinking straight, Ro. I was worried sick."

I was angry, although knew I should not have been. "I have to call him."

"He's on his way over. He can take you home."

"I'm not going home," I snapped. "You need me here at work. Cara's taken everything from me, she's not going to take this place, too."

I stared at her, hard, silently daring her to argue.

"Cara," she said, her eyes narrowing. "How did I know she had something to do with this?"

"It's none of your business."

"I'm not angry at you, Ro, but if I see her again, I'll ..."

"It doesn't matter. None of it matters. Please, just let me work the rest of the day through and I promise when I come in tomorrow, I'll have a clear head."

"Whatever she did to you, Ro, it wasn't your fault."

"Will everyone stop telling me how nice a person I am? Would everyone stop telling me I'm a swell kid and I could never be mean or snide or intentionally step on an ant or something? I'm not a good person, Jas, I'm not a sweet and innocent girl. I'm a ... a ..."

She waited. "You're a what, Ro?"

I took a deep breath to calm myself. "I'm going to call Dad and tell him not to worry. I let those people on the beach get to me and I shouldn't have. That's all it was."

"You want me to call him?"

"No, I'll do it."

So I called him. Dad wasn't happy that I was telling him to turn around and go home, but I convinced him there was no need to come get me. Or at least I asked him not to before passing the phone over to Jasmine, who promised to watch out for me for the rest of the day.

"Thank you," I said once we hung up. I meant to say it sincerely but it came out glibly instead.

"Ro, put your clothes on, sit down and eat your sandwiches. Once you've done that, you can get back to work. If you don't eat your sandwiches, I'm calling your father again, I swear."

I sat in a sulk and ate my sandwiches. Then I got dressed. I wasn't sure, but there was a chance I did it in that order just to defy her.

I worked hard for the rest of the day. I tried to put Cara from my mind, just so I could show Jasmine I was feeling better, but I had not eaten properly and the heat of the day was frazzling my brain. By the time we closed the shop, I had begun to fool her, but there was no fooling myself.

I promised Jasmine I would go straight home and she said she believed me. But I lied. I had no intention of going straight home, for I needed to clear my head. Instead, I went to the pier. Why I did that, I had no idea, although perhaps it was because the pier had become such an intrinsic part of my life that I could not stand the thought of Cara taking that from me as well. Cara had not been the first date I had had on the pier. Some had ended well, some badly, but I had never avoided the place afterwards.

The thought of going all the way to the back, to visit Sophie in *The Mermaid*, filled me with dread, so I hung around the games and the shops. I watched young couples at the shooting gallery, I saw a teenage boy win a teddy at hook-a-duck for his girlfriend, I heard the joyful screams of people on the rollercoaster up above and I watched friendly rivalry being played out in the bumper cars.

The pier was as it always had been. I had both good memories and bad from all of those things, and I refused to let anything get in the way of my love for the place.

Proud of my resolve, I inhaled deeply and strode back down the pier. I would go home, I would be strong enough to explain things to my father and beg his forgiveness. Who was going to tell my sister, I had no idea. She was a year younger than me and I had always been her idol. I had no clue as to how she would react.

Passing a shop on the pier, I found my eyes drawn to something. It was a small place which sold goods similar to those we sold, although they concentrated more on the trinket side of things. In their doorway was a rack of postcards and sitting in several slots was an image with a pinkish-brown background and a young woman in a blue swimsuit twisting her body and pouting for the camera. Beneath the image were emblazoned the words 'The Captain's Bombshell'.

Suddenly, I understood how the people on the beach had seen the image of me. They had not been looking on the Internet, they had not been perusing top-shelf magazines. They had simply come from the pier and had bought a postcard.

My family would not have to access the Internet to find the pictures; all they had to do was take a stroll down the pier, or look in any seaside shop that sold postcards.

I emitted a near-silent shriek as I thought of Jasmine. Then my heart began to beat again when I remembered I had spent the morning getting rid of our postcards because they no longer sold. Jasmine was having a delivery in the morning, but there would not be any postcards. After all, since they did not sell, she would not have asked for any new ones.

Except she had said she had forgotten to tell them not to include any. That meant tomorrow morning, Jasmine's delivery would turn up with boxes of postcards, all with my image.

I stumbled along the pier, all sense of reason gone. My energy reserves were low, my hope was dying and I had no idea how to stop this. I reached out a hand as I felt my knees go and caught the railing at the side of the pier. Falling to my knees, I breathed heavily, forcing air into my lungs as I vainly tried to work out what to do. I was vaguely aware of people around me. Some were asking if I was all right, others were condemning me for being drunk. No one was connecting me to the Captain's Bombshell, although at the back of the crowd I could see someone holding the postcard with a view to buying it. She looked over at me with a frown, looked down to the card and said something to the man she was with.

I was up and gone in an instant. I fled from the pier, angry I had allowed it to affect me so much, angrier still that this was yet one more thing Cara had taken from me.

I went home, revealed nothing to my father and rushed up to my room to cry into my pillow.

It seemed all my old routines were gone and I was already developing new ones.

# CHAPTER EIGHT

The following morning, I left early for work, although first pulled myself together for the sake of my father. Whether my sister knew I spent most of my time at home crying was something I could not say, but I wanted Dad to think I was over my troubles. I even managed to remember to take my lunch. When he asked me why I was going into work so early, I told him we had a big delivery that morning and I wanted to make up to Jasmine for being such a worry. I was getting my priorities straight, I told him. I was behaving like an adult.

He had replied by ruffling my hair and telling me I would always be his little girl.

The sun was up when I got to work, although in Glazton it never seemed to get dark in the summertime. I opened up the shop – Jasmine had long ago given me a key – and got everything ready. Thanks to my work the previous day, there was plenty of space to put all the new stock, so all I had to do was wait for it to arrive. My plan was to find all the postcards and destroy them; then fill up the shelves with the new items so that when Jasmine arrived, she would see all the hard work I had done. She would never know there were any postcards in the work order and would be happy I was back to my usual self.

Half an hour later, I was still waiting for the delivery and I was beginning to panic. Jasmine had not said what time it would arrive, but I had assumed it would have been around an hour before we opened up the shop. I paced outside, keeping a constant vigil for any trucks on the road on the slight hill just behind the shop. If Jasmine arrived before the delivery, all my plans would be ruined.

Ten minutes later, I was trying to find some paperwork from the suppliers so I could call them and ask when they would turn up. If there was any such paperwork on-site, however, it would have been in the locked cabinet behind the counter, and I did not have a key for that.

Just when I thought I would tear out my hair in despair, I heard an engine and saw a van pulling up. Forcing myself not to race to meet them, I stayed with the shop while I watched the delivery woman doing something with her paperwork in the cabin. Then she played with her phone a bit; then she hunted around for a mint; then she got out of the van and went round the back. After a while, she opened the rear doors; then she went back inside the van for some more paperwork. Then she made a phone call.

At that point, I decided to wait in the shop and count to a thousand.

I did not quite get that far before I heard her trundling along with a pallet of boxes. She was pulling it on one of those strange metal contraptions which look like two skis stuck together and operated by a massive winch.

"One delivery for you," she said, handing over some paperwork. "If you could sign your life away, I'll get these set down for you."

I signed, not reading the thing, and helped her unload the pallet. She said there was no need but I did it anyway and I don't think I said a word to her. After an eternity, she departed and I hastily tore open the boxes in search of postcards.

There were twenty boxes in all and most contained uninflated beach-balls, towels, kites and other similar items. I would deal with those later, once I had found and destroyed the postcards. The next box I opened was filled with carefully packed glass models of seahorses and tubby sailors. They were different fare to what we usually sold and perhaps they would do well, but they were not what I was interested in.

Ripping open the next box, I at last found the postcards. My relief flooded through my pores and left moist patches on the cardboard box. Quickly sorting through the postcards, I found several different styles but none with my image on them. Each style was wrapped separately and I rooted through them until I caught a glimpse of blue. With shaking hands, I removed the stash of offensive postcards from the box and quickly checked to make sure there were no other bundles in there.

It was a thick wad containing probably fifty and I realised I had not thought how I was going to destroy them.

Using my teeth, I tore away the outer wrapper and my nervous fingers dropped them to the ground. The wind caught them and I panicked, but I stamped on them before they could blow away. Collecting them, I had not lost a single one and took them into the shop. On the counter, we sold novelty lighters, and the most effective way of destroying cardboard was to burn it out of existence. There was a metal bucket beneath the counter – probably a relic from when sand used to be tipped onto flames to douse them – and I placed all the postcards in this. I held one in my hand and looked at the vulgar image. The flirtatious girl on the card was a monstrous image whose pout almost pleaded with me not to harm her. Taking up a lighter, I betrayed no emotion as I sparked the light and set the flame to the edge of the card.

The flame took easily to the card and I watched the girl scream as she was devoured. Once I had a fair-sized fireball in my hand, I dropped it into the metal bucket and poked and prodded the cards with my fingers until they were all burning. My fingers were throbbing with pain and my nails were turning black, but I had to destroy them. I had to burn the vile things away.

"Rowena, what the hell are you doing?"

I spun, not having heard Jasmine approach. She stared at me in horror and for a moment I thought she had seen the postcards, but it was not the cards which had caused her to look at me that way. I stood in the shop, holding a lighter, a fire raging in the bucket before me, with boxes strewn around the floor outside, their lids torn off, their contents being battered by the sea winds.

"I can explain," I said.

"I'm waiting. We can't afford to lose this stock. If this is damaged, we're going under. Today. Right now."

"I ... I ..."

"What are you burning? Why are you setting fires in my shop?"

She grabbed the bucket but there were still portions of the cards which had yet to curl and die. Distraught, I snatched it back off her and we tugged the bucket back and forth, the fire heating the metal and threatening to spill over into the shop.

"Rowena, let go."

"No." I shoved forward with the bucket, knocking Jasmine backwards. The force tipped the bucket over and the remains of the cards tipped across the floor, landing on one of the boxes. The metal bucket clanged as it struck the floor and I scrabbled to make sure all the cards were destroyed. Unfortunately, the flames had caught the box and I grabbed it, yanking it up hard. The box came halfway up before the remains of the lid tore in my grip and the box overturned.

A great crash resounded through the shop as the precious glass ornaments shattered.

I stared, dumbfounded. Around me, the postcards had turned to ashes and Jasmine was busy stamping out what remained of the fire, but glass shards littered the floor. They had looked so expensive.

"Explain," Jasmine shouted once she was done stamping out the flames. "Explain to me why you just tore open all my stock and broke the one range of things that might have saved us." She was furious, and there were tears forming in her eyes. I knew then the true damage I had done, for Jasmine had spent all her money on those things. They were her last-ditch effort to save the shop and I had destroyed them.

"I'm sorry," I said.

"You're sorry?"

I reached out to pick up something, to salvage something, but Jasmine knocked my hand away.

"Broken glass," she said. "What are you going to do anyway? Piece them back together with your tears?"

"I'm sorry."

"You said that already. It doesn't change anything. Rowena, I've tried to be patient, I've tried to be understanding. You broke up with a woman you just met. You went on a date and it didn't work out. Deal with it. It's what adults do. Instead, you mope around and now ... now this."

"I'm sorry," I said, my fist in my mouth where I fought to stop myself from trembling.

"Stop saying you're sorry!" she shouted. "We've all been where you are, Rowena, we just didn't all act like stupid kids over it."

"You don't understand."

"So tell me. Tell me right now what's wrong with you. Tell me or you're done."

"I can't."

"Then that's it. You're fired."

My eyes widened.

"Get out. Go on. Let me deal with this mess. Maybe I can salvage something if I don't have to pay you any more."

"Jasmine, I ..."

"Go!"

I wanted to say something more, wanted to tell her everything, but even that would not have done any good. I had already ruined all her stock; telling her of my shame would not make her think any better of me.

Hanging my head, I walked away from the shop. It was all I had left and now that was gone as well. But it was not just that. I had ruined things for Jasmine. With a little luck and a lot of hard work, she could have saved the shop. Thanks to me, she no longer had a chance to do that.

The only lives I had yet to ruin were those of my family, and I knew that would not be long coming. I could keep the postcards out of their way for only so long; and after that, they would discover the other images. Once the Captain's Bombshell got into my family's lives, one of them would discover the topless photos as well. I still did not know where they had been published, whether in a magazine or on the Internet – perhaps both – but it did not matter. Wherever they were, they would be found.

In trying to forestall the inevitable, I had ended Jasmine's business. She hated me; but it was nothing compared to how much I hated myself.

# CHAPTER NINE

It was still early in the morning and the beach was not busy, which allowed me to wander in silence. I'd left my bag back at the shop and had only the clothes on my back, but I no longer even had all of those because I'd tossed away my shoes in order to walk barefoot through the surf. The waves were cold, almost icy that early in the morning. They were either mocking me by slapping at me before retreating, else they were caressing my feet and trying to make me feel better. Either way, they could not change what I had done, could not erase the plethora of mistakes I was continually heaping upon anyone I cared about.

I had no destination in mind, but then nor did I have a reason to do anything. I could not return home, for my father would be there and he would not only be upset but disappointed. Even if I revealed to him the entire truth, it would not make up for having destroyed Jasmine's business. Dad would call me a stupid, spoiled little girl. He would shout at me for the disgrace I was and he would hate me.

Perhaps he had already found out about the pictures, or at the very least maybe Jasmine had called him and told him I had been fired. Perhaps he was already hating me.

No, I could not go home.

I could not go home, could not go to work and could not talk to my friends, for they had all moved away. I thought then of Sophie, but could only imagine her reaction. She had never liked Cara – of everyone in my life, it had been Sophie who had seen the most of her. Sophie had known what Cara was like and she would be expecting me to go to her with news like this.

All I had left was the beach. When it began to fill up, I would not even have that, for sooner or later someone would recognise me and I would run away again to weep in a locked cubicle.

I sank to my knees in the surf and faced the sea. I debated whether to stay there, to lie on the beach and wait for the tide to come in. Would the sea even want me? Or would it spit me out, or collect me under the pier along with all the other waste and litter people tossed into the water?

"Please," I said to the sea, for I had no other friend. "Please, just tell me what to do. I don't know what to do." The only answer was the roar of laughter and I hung my head in resignation.

The waves came in slowly until they no longer caressed me to dart away again. My feet were under the water, as were my legs up to my knees where I was kneeling. My trousers were soaked through and I was cold; but I deserved to be cold.

I must have stayed that way for an hour, but the sea did not claim me. It rose past my knees but it would be a long time before it stole me entirely, and by then families would have taken to the beach in their droves and no one wanted their children to watch as the sea took someone from the shore.

Rising, I brushed the sand off my trousers and resumed my walk through the surf. I was even colder now I was out of the water, with the biting chill of the wind stabbing at me, and I shivered uncontrollably. Before long, a shadow fell across the beach ahead and I looked up to find I had made it to the pier. Somehow, I had been walking in entirely the opposite direction to what I had thought, which meant I was close to the shop, where I had begun. I looked over, straining to see, and could make out Jasmine behind the till. She was serving a customer, although even from my distance I could see there was not a lot of stock on sale. The shelves were bare where we had removed some items to make room for the glass ornaments, and with nothing to replace them it was hardly worth having opened the shop at all.

Jasmine was now working damage control. At the end of the summer, she would have to close, but was fighting to make sure her debt to the bank was as low as it could be. The thing about debt, of course, was that it did not matter how low it started off, for it would quickly spiral into something crippling. Jasmine would file for bankruptcy and her chances of ever running a business again would be gone.

I found myself on the pier without even realising I had walked there. The shop was behind me now, I would never return to it. Keeping my eyes low, I strolled across the pier, the joyous sounds already having begun. There were not many people enjoying the games and the sugary treats, but that would all change as the morning wore on. The shops were all open and I paused as I passed the rack of postcards, where my damaging image was displayed for all the world to see.

My mind turned as it always did to those other pictures. If I could just find where the nude shots had been published, I would at least know what I would have to hide. It was the not knowing which was hurting the most, for every time I looked in someone's eyes, I wondered whether they had seen them.

Someone came by and turned the rack in order to select a card and I lowered my eyes again and hastened on.

The woman running the hook-a-duck was calling for customers and I stopped, for this was where we had won the bear. Seeing my interest, the woman encouraged me to try. "Everyone's a winner," she said.

"No," I replied. "Not everyone."

I walked on to where the man at the shooting gallery was drumming up trade. He did not notice me, for I was careful not to show any interest, yet I remembered being proud of how good Cara was at firing the rifle.

I came to the bumper cars, in which two children were happily bumping each other and laughing at their antics while their worried parents looked on. I had not been happy with the ride myself, had found it the least intimate thing I had ever done on a date. It seemed it was just the first in a series of ways Cara had battered me and I should have taken it as a sign.

That I was stupid explained a lot. Everyone thought I was naïve, but that was not true. I was simply an idiot.

At the end of the pier was *The Mermaid* and I walked in without meaning to. There were only a few people there, for it was still very early. I approached the bar and there was someone working there I did not recognise.

"Is Sophie on yet?" I asked.

"No, sorry," the young woman said. "Can I get you something?"

"You can get me Sophie."

"I can't get you Sophie. She's probably in bed."

"Is Frank here?"

"No, he's probably in bed with her. Are you friends with them?"

I felt my heart tremble but refused to cry. "I need to talk with her."

"Then call her, if you're her friend. But not right now, because she's in bed."

I had not thought of that. I could phone Sophie. She would tell me I was an idiot and that she had warned me against dating Cara, but I could live with that. I needed to talk with someone; if my long walk across the beach had taught me one thing, it was that I needed to talk with someone.

I patted myself down and realised my phone was in my bag, which was in the shop. "I don't have my phone," I said.

"Then come back at midday. That's when her shift starts."

I glanced at my watch, but that was also in my bag. "Do you know what the time is?"

"Half nine."

"Half nine?" I could not wait two and a half hours to see Sophie, yet it seemed I would have to.

I wandered back across the bar while I tried to work out what to do. Behind me, I heard the woman mutter, "You're welcome," and knew I had managed to offend someone else.

Back on the pier, I still had no destination. I would have to kill two and a half hours, but then what could I really say to Sophie? Nothing I could say would solve anything – it was not as though Sophie was my fairy godmother or had a magic wand or something. All I could say was that I should have listened to her, that she was right and that I was the most useless human being in existence.

Strolling beyond *The Mermaid*, I reached the end of the pier. The metal railings stopped people from falling into the water, and I stood there leaning against them, staring out into the depths of the sea. Formed of two thick horizontal bars, the railings were old but sturdy. The winds were wild, for the pier stretched farther out to sea than people often imagined. My legs were freezing where they were wet and my hair slapped me as though trying to hide my shameful face. Either that or it was attacking me. Whichever was the truth, my hair was right to do it.

"It's probably a drunk," my words echoed in my head when Cara and I had been standing at the railing overlooking the sea. We had seen the lifeboat speeding away to save someone and I was filling Cara in on how life at the seaside worked. "They fall in from time to time. They cause no end of problems for the lifeguards."

"People fall in the sea when they're drunk? Why do they put a bar on the pier, then? Drown your sorrows then drown yourself."

Her words were terrible, yet I recalled them all. Again, it was another clue as to her true nature. Another clue I should have noticed.

"I just think anyone stupid enough to fall in the sea after drinking deserves to drown," she had said. It was a disgusting attitude and insulted the good work our lifeguards did.

The rest of Cara's words rang through my brain, as though carried by the wind and taunting me.

"If life's so bad that you have to jump in the sea," she had said, "then you should just die and get it over with."

My foot was on the first horizontal railing before I had finished the thought and I stopped. Life was bad, yes, but horror flooded through me at the very notion of what I was doing. Life was bad, but I had almost jumped into the sea. Cara had controlled my life right up until the point she had vanished, and she continued to control it even after she was gone. I would not allow her to control my death as well.

"If life's so bad that you have to jump in the sea, then you should just die and get it over with."

"No," I said to the wind. "It's not. My family ..." would be disappointed. They would despise me and be so ashamed it would break my poor father's heart. "Jasmine ..." wanted nothing more to do with me. I had ruined her life and forced her into such massive debt she would never recover. "Sophie ..." would hug me and tell me everything would be all right. It would be a lie. Finally, with grief choking my throat, I said, "Cara ..." had used me, abused me and abandoned me.

The wind howled with laughter, for it understood my heart and soul were damned. The wind knew all, as did the sea. There was a saying in Glazton: the only constant in life is the sea. The tides came in, the tides went out. Holes dug were washed over, litter disposed of was washed ashore. Water covered two third of the globe and laughed at the land even as it eroded it. Eventually, the Earth would no doubt be one great ball of ocean and the sea would stop laughing only because it no longer had anyone to laugh at.

In the wind, I could hear Cara's voice. Over and over, it echoed in my brain.

"If life's so bad that you have to jump in the sea," she had said, "then you should just die and get it over with."

She was right. Life was bad.

My other foot left the ground. After that, I had no awareness of what I was doing. I thought of Sophie, of Jasmine. I thought of my sister. I thought of my father; most of all I thought of my father, who had always loved me and who had never judged. My father was my hero and I had always been his little girl.

I was no longer that little girl and could not face my hero's disappointment.

I did not think of Cara at all, for she was already dead to me. Just as I wanted to be dead to the world.

The water was hard as I struck it, and cold. Beyond that, I knew nothing, for in that moment I did what I wholly deserved to do – I died.

# CHAPTER TEN

I awoke, gasping for air. My arms flailed, my chest heaved and I spat water where I lay on my back. There were people around me, vague ghostly forms I could not quite make out. I could hear, as well, for there was a lot of commotion. Someone cheered, and I hated them for it. I closed my eyes and someone shook me to keep me awake. I swore at them, something I had never done before, and attempted a half-hearted slap, but my energy was spent and I lay there breathing hard.

Time passed, I did not know how long. It may have been a few minutes, might well have been an hour or more. During that time, my mind churned with conflicting emotions, but chief among them was disappointment. Disappointment that I could not even die right.

"Hey, Ro."

I opened my eyes to find I was in a cabin of some sort. There were windows overlooking the sea and life-jackets hanging on the walls. There was rope in the cabin, and symbols I recognised as belonging to the lifeguards. There was someone at the back of the cabin, sitting behind a desk and filling in paperwork, but it was the woman sitting beside me who had spoken.

I was grateful for it not being my father.

"Ro," Jasmine said, "how are you feeling?"

"I'm sorry," I said. "Jasmine, I'm so sorry."

"You fell."

I closed my eyes and said nothing.

"You didn't fall," Jasmine said, afraid. It was not a question.

"I didn't fall," I said, my voice small, weak – broken.

Neither of us said anything for several moments. All I could hear was the familiar crash of the waves outside. I loved the sea, I had always loved the sea. It was where I felt safe, where nothing could harm me.

My throat was tight at the thought of what I had done.

"Can I take her home?" Jasmine asked.

I opened my eyes to see she had moved over to the woman at the desk. The woman clearly worked for the Lifeboat Institution and she did not look happy.

"She swallowed a lot of water," the woman said. "She really should go to hospital."

"I'll take care of her."

The woman glanced at me and in her eyes I could see disdain. "Sure. No sense in her wasting the time of another emergency service."

Jasmine dealt with the necessary paperwork, or at least that was what I assumed she was doing. While she was doing that, I swung my legs over the side of whatever it was I was lying on. It was a table with a towel over the top. I noticed then I was no longer wearing my clothes; instead, I was dressed in white shorts and a white T-shirt. Neither was my size, but I could hardly complain.

Getting shakily to my feet, I held the table for support while I waited for Jasmine.

"Take it easy," Jasmine said. She took me by the shoulders but I gently shook her away. I was still struggling to come to terms with what I had done, but inside I felt numb. A massive part of me still had yet to understand what had happened, and the only image I could focus on was my father's face, looking disappointed as he shook his head.

"Let's get you out of here," Jasmine said kindly.

"Jas, the shop. It's daylight, you should be ..."

"The shop's not important, Ro. You are. Now let's get you home."

The thought of going home filled me with dread. "No," I said, my heart racing. "No, I can't go home. My dad'll kill me."

"I very much doubt that."

"Jas, please. Please, I ..." I held her by the arms but my fingers were so cold I had no idea how much pressure I was exerting. My body was numb but pain filled my heart. "Please, I can't go home."

"I'll take you back to my place." She looked to the lifeguard. "Thanks for all your help."

"Yes," I said to her. "Thank you. I'm sorry for all the trouble."

"I'm used to it," the woman grumbled.

"You shouldn't be. You shouldn't have to risk your lives to save idiots."

The woman's expression softened a little at my words, as though she was confused. "Couldn't agree more."

"Ro?" Jasmine said.

I looked back to her, realised I was still clinging to her arm. Her eyes were wide and fearful. Jasmine may have been my boss, but she was also my best friend. "Jas, I'm so sorry."

I collapsed into her arms and cried. She held me patiently, her hand on my back the most secure thing in my entire life. "It'll be all right, Ro. I promise, it'll be all right."

She had her car waiting outside and I buckled myself into the passenger seat. Jasmine did not talk while we drove, although I knew the lecture would come as soon as we got to her place. I was ready for it, I deserved it, and I promised myself I would take it without crying. I had been doing so much of that lately, it was as though I was trying to create my very own ocean.

We arrived at her house and Jasmine helped me out of the car, although I wanted to walk under my own steam. Her house was smaller than mine, but then she lived alone and did not need much space. I had been there before and she always made me feel welcome. One time, she had let me crash at her place when I had broken up with a girlfriend. I had been too emotional to go home and had phoned her to cry at her down the line. She had not only allowed me to stay over, but she had also phoned my father for me to explain things, had made me a dinner which I had not eaten, and breakfast which I did.

She was a wonderful woman and I had abused her trust by smashing those glass statues. Now she was losing a precious day's work, and all because I had been selfish enough to hurl myself into the sea.

I sat on the settee in her cosy living-room. She had a television, a cabinet where she displayed her collection of model pigs – Jasmine loved pigs and had made something of an obsession out of them. There were not many personal touches to her living-room, and there were no pictures of her family. The only photograph was in a small frame and sat next to the TV. It was of both of us from two years earlier, about a year after she had first given me a job. We were sitting on the beach, with sunglasses and huge smiles plastered to our faces. I had an ice cream on my head, the stickiness running through my red hair. For the life of me, I could not recall why I had an ice cream on my head, but it had been a fantastic time.

Her cupboard held books and DVDs, while on her coffee table was a half-eaten box of chocolates.

I was reminded of my kiss with Cara on the beach. She had brought so much odd food to our picnic that her lips and tongue had tasted of chocolate. It was the first time I had thought of Cara since waking up and I shuddered at the thought of ever allowing that woman to kiss me.

"Here," Jasmine said, returning to the living-room to sit on the other end of the settee. There was a space between us, which she was purposefully leaving so I would not feel confined. She handed me a steaming mug, which I gratefully accepted. I was still shaking and my bones were freezing. The heat of the mug infused my body, but the smell only dredged up those bad memories all over again.

"Hot chocolate," I said.

"You love hot chocolate."

I sipped it. The taste on my tongue was bitter, although the heat as it slid down my throat was soothing. I took another sip and refused to allow Cara to ruin chocolate for me as well.

"Thank you," I said flatly. "For everything."

Jasmine shrugged.

"You must hate me," I said.

"Why would I hate you?"

"Y'know."

"Because you burned my stock? Because you broke my glass ornaments? Or because you tried to kill yourself by jumping off the pier?"

I winced, not looking at her. It was not until the words had been spoken aloud that they were truly sinking in. My stomach churned with what I had done and I knew I would vomit if I was not careful. It seemed I was doing a lot of that lately, as well.

"You should eat something," Jasmine said. "What do you fancy?"

"Nothing."

"Ro, I'm not taking no for an answer on this."

I said nothing.

"All right. We'll talk first; then you'll eat."

I took another sip of hot chocolate, although it still tasted bitter.

"I haven't called your father," she said. "I'll leave you to tell him, but I think you should."

"Tell him I jumped off the pier?"

"You have problems, Ro. I don't know how to help you. Maybe you need to talk to someone."

"I'm talking to you."

"I meant a shrink."

"I'm not seeing a shrink."

"Then talk to me. You say you're talking to me, but you're not saying anything. Rowena, you're in a really bad place right now and I want to help you. I want to do whatever I can to help you, but I can't do that if you won't let me in."

I looked up to her then. She was hurting, just like my father had been when I had been staring into my cereal. It seemed I was so wrapped up in my problems that I had long ago stopped taking into consideration how everyone else in my life felt.

"OK," Jasmine said, shifting position on the settee. She placed her elbow against the back and crossed her legs so she could look at me better. "If you're not going to talk, I will. The Captain's Bombshell."

I swore in terror and astonishment; I may even have used the F-word but I had no idea what I was saying so could not be sure.

Jasmine kept her eyes levelled upon me. "After the incident this morning," she said, "I tidied up the shop and swept up the broken glass. But first I called my suppliers. I can't afford to replace the glass statues, but I wanted to know what it was you were burning. I still hadn't calmed down by that point, but I figured if I could see whatever it was, I might understand you a little better. I looked at the barcode on the wrapper they were in and gave them the serial number. They told me it had been a set of postcards and I asked for a replacement batch to be sent urgently. They arrived within the hour. I had to pay more for that, but it was worth it just to find out what was going on."

"You've seen them?"

"Yeah. I've seen them." She produced something from her pocket and unfolded it before dropping it onto the settee between us. I did not need to look at it to know it was a postcard. "At first I was confused," she said. "I was still angry, but it wasn't what I'd expected. To be honest, I hadn't known what to expect, but that most certainly hadn't been it. If you'd posed for a postcard, I couldn't understand why you'd be burning them. I mean, it's a cute photo. You're a very moral person, but there's nothing immoral about it. If you want to make some extra money while you're young by flaunting what you've got, where's the problem? And, cards on the table here, you do have it. In spades." She paused. "Little seaside joke there, like bucket and spades?"

I did not laugh.

She sighed heavily – a sure sign she was still trying to work me out.

"When I got over my anger," she continued, "I worked through my confusion. There's nothing wrong with posing in a swimsuit. There must be a lot of money in doing it. That you'd done it surprised me, since you've always been so reserved. Your family life means everything to you and I couldn't imagine you'd think your father would be happy with you being a pin-up girl.

"Then I realised the piece of the puzzle I was missing. You're a strong person, Ro, you always stand your ground and you always do what's right. You've never let yourself get talked into anything. You don't drink, you don't smoke, you don't touch drugs. You're the girl next door everyone would be proud to take home to their folks. So what could have made you pose for photos like that? Money? You don't have any, so you couldn't have been paid for them.

"Love. Love is your weakness, Ro, it always has been. You're trusting and you're loving and, to be frank, it makes you gullible. The missing piece was Cara. Tell me I'm wrong."

The chocolate in my cup was shaking, which meant I must have been as well, although I was too dead inside to know for certain. "Yes," I said in a small voice.

"Ro, would you please talk to me? I can fit things together myself, but it'd be better if you just told me what's going on."

"She's a photographer. I was going to show her around town so she could shoot some pictures." I inhaled deeply to clear my brain, perhaps to give me strength enough to say the rest. "She asked me to pose for her, said it would give her employers a feel of the seaside. She said they'd be for her portfolio, that she wouldn't sell any of them. She said it would help convince them to keep her here all through the summer. She said we'd be together."

"She seems to have said a lot of things, Ro, but kept none of her promises."

"We kissed. On the beach. It was wonderful. But she was using me. Everything she did, everything she said, it was all to get me into her studio so she could take the pictures."

"What she's done is illegal. Or at least it should be. No, it has to be. Selling pictures of you without your consent, without you making any money, has to be illegal. I take it you didn't receive any money?"

"No."

"Or sign a contract?"

"No."

"Then we'll contact the police and have her arrested."

I knew I should have felt better for having talked about it with someone, but the truth was I didn't. "I'm sorry for all the trouble I've caused," I said, still staring into my drink.

"You haven't caused any trouble, Ro. It's this Cara that's caused all the trouble. You're just you and you'll always be you. And it makes me furious that she's hurt you like this."

There was no answer I could give to that.

"Ro, look at the picture."

"No."

"Ro, look at the picture."

I slowly turned my head to look at the crumpled postcard sitting on the settee. It was creased down the middle but even half folded it was enough to make my heart thump.

"There's nothing wrong with it," Jasmine said. "In principal, yes. She tricked you into letting her take the picture, but there's nothing wrong with the actual picture. When your family finds out, they're going to be confused, but you just have to tell them what happened. You have to tell them you were deceived, and they'll understand. Besides, it's just you in a swimsuit. I know you're heartbroken over this, but it could have been a lot worse."

My eyes rose from the picture and I looked at her. "It is," I said. "She convinced me …" I took another deep breath. "She took … She …" I took another one, but it did not help. "I did some topless photos for her.

She took a hundred pictures, maybe more. Me undressing, me touching my chest, me …" I closed my eyes briefly but the memories were burned into my soul. "She has a lot of photos of me, Jas, and when my father sees them it'll kill him."

Jasmine did not reply and I watched her for several moments. She was staring at something across the room and I followed her gaze. She was looking at a photo sitting on her cupboard. It was not framed and it was partially tucked away behind a pig ornament, but it was there none the less. It was something I had seen before: a photo of Jasmine on stage back in her days of amateur acting.

"You didn't do anything wrong," she said at last. "You're a victim. If you ever forget that, you'll end up in the sea again, or you'll open up your wrists or … something."

"Something?" I asked.

"Something." It was Jasmine's turn to inhale deeply. "When I was younger, I wanted to be an actress."

"I know. You're great, you would have made a fine actress."

"I thought so, too. I just needed someone to notice me. We met every night to practise for whatever play we were putting out, and they were always amazing. The crowds were great, the applause the most wonderful thing I'd ever experienced. I loved my acting days, but the theatre is a difficult thing to get into and all we were doing was amateur dramatics. We weren't being noticed.

"One day, I was sitting in a park, feeding the squirrels and trying to work out how I could make something of myself. This guy came by. I was fifteen, he was forty-seven. He said he'd seen me the night before in our production of Othello, said I was fabulous."

"The newspaper cutting," I said. "You played Desdemona."

"That was what made me believe him. The paper had printed that article the day before and my head was swelled with pride and promise. So when this man approached me on the bench and said he was a director looking for the next big thing, I believed him. I didn't ask enough questions, didn't want to know the real answers. I didn't stop to think he wasn't a director and that he'd just read the same article I had."

I had a feeling I knew where her story was going but did not interrupt.

"He said he wanted to take me out for dinner," Jasmine continued. "I was fifteen, I said, so I'd have to check with my folks. He laughed at that, said he'd look me up when I considered myself an adult. So I went with him, said I didn't have to talk to my folks at all. He took me to a fancy restaurant, we had lobster. I remember he had trouble with it and I had to show him how to eat it. During dinner, he said all the right things, and my answers were apparently perfect.

"It was dark by the time we left the restaurant and I said I needed to get home. He said he'd made the decision to hire me but that he needed to hear me read for the part. I told him I needed to call my parents, that they'd be worried sick. He laughed and said if I didn't read for the role that night, he'd give it to some other girl.

"We got a taxi back to his hotel. He gave me the script and I read it with gusto. There was no one else around, so he read the part of the male lead. We worked through the whole thing, it was a saucy piece about a man cheating on his wife with a fifteen-year-old girl. By the end, he said he was pleased with my performance but that we needed to get into the spirit of things.

"I don't have to go into details, Ro. The script called for him to take off my shirt, then my underwear. I wasn't happy with it, but I couldn't let the role go to someone else. It was acting, I told myself, it wasn't real. We kissed, but that wasn't real, either. Then, of course, there was the lovemaking scene. It was pretend, he said, we had to emulate the enjoyment. So we ..." She closed her eyes and when she opened them again her face was stone. "He wasn't even apologetic afterward, although he did admit he'd got carried away. I felt sick, but at the same time was worried he'd cast someone else because I wasn't good enough. It was my first time, obviously – I was fifteen. He asked me what I was complaining about, told me to grow up and stop being childish. Then he said we needed to perfect that scene, that I needed to be comfortable. I told him no, that we wouldn't be literally having sex on stage, but he argued that it was the best way to feel comfortable.

"The more I refused, the angrier he became. The angrier he became, the more I was confused. I didn't want to lose the role, I didn't want to allow what I had already sacrificed to be in vain. So we did the scene again. This time I actually was sick and something awoke inside me, something which screamed at me to realise what I was doing.

"He drove me home, said he'd call me, but by this time I was barely listening. He had fooled me into having sex with him; but the second time ... the second time was because I was selfish, because I wanted to succeed. I wanted to make him happy so he'd take me on in his play and I'd sold myself for that.

"I didn't tell anyone. I couldn't. If it was just the once, I could maybe have told my folks, but I was aware of what I was doing the second time, I told myself. I was a whore, there was no other word for me.

"Needless to say, I never heard from him again.

"My secret stayed with me for a while. It didn't stay a secret forever. I started feeling strange: nausea and all of that. My mother took me to the doctor and it turned out I was pregnant. I was still fifteen.

"I had an abortion before the baby could get too far along, but I could never tell my parents what had happened. I was too ashamed of what I'd become. After that, my father became depressed. The following year he had a heart attack and died. My mother hasn't spoken to me since.

"I took a lot of pills that night. I went to every pharmacy I could find and bought the maximum amount of pills you can in one go. I don't even know how many boxes I had, but I sat on that same park bench with a bottle of vodka and downed the lot of them.

"Next morning, I woke up in the hospital. The doctor told me my mother had been called. I was in the hospital for three days and she never came."

I did not know what to say. As bad as Cara had been to me, my tale of woe was nothing compared with Jasmine's.

"It took me a long time," she said, "to come to terms with what had happened. I was a victim, Ro. I was a stupid fifteen-year-old with dreams of the future. Doesn't matter if you're fifteen or twenty-two; if you have dreams and hopes, you'd do anything to achieve them. That's all you were doing, Ro, trying to realise your dreams. This woman took advantage of that, she took advantage of you. You're not at fault here. These postcards, the nude images … none of it's your fault. Talking doesn't solve the problem, but it doesn't hurt, either."

"Jas, I never knew."

"I never told you. It's not a story I tell people. And by that, I mean it's not a story I've ever told anyone."

"No one?"

She shook her head.

"Talking doesn't solve the problem," I told her, "but it doesn't hurt, either."

She smiled, although her eyes were still in pain. Setting down my mug, I reached across the settee and hugged her. She was startled at first, but moments later returned my hug. We sat there for some time, both of us openly weeping over what we had been through, what we had suffered, and I think I was crying more for my friend than I was for myself.

When we had no more tears to shed, we pulled away and Jasmine said, "You're staying here tonight.

I'll call your father. Don't worry, I won't go into detail, but I'll tell him I know what's wrong and that you need some space for a while."

"What if he finds out I tried to kill myself?"

"Not from me he won't. All he'll know is that you're safe and that you have someone who's going to help you."

"Help me?"

"Yes. We're not taking this lying down, Rowena. I'm going to cook you something and you're going to eat it. Then we'll play a few rounds of Ludo, because it's your favourite game and it'll help you relax. Then you're going to get a good night's sleep because you're going to be minding the shop by yourself for most of tomorrow."

"I'm not fired any more?"

"Of course you're not fired any more."

"Hold on, mind the shop? Where will you be?"

"I have an errand to run."

I was not sure I liked the sound of that, but for the first time in a while, my heart was filled with hope. I did not press for details. Instead I drank my hot chocolate while Jasmine made me a lasagne. Then we played Ludo for an hour before we finally went to bed. Jasmine's house may have been small, but she always kept the spare bed made up in case she had guests. That night, as I lay on my back, I thought of how lonely she must have been, how her experience had scarred her and that it had probably been the main contributing factor for why she had never married. In all the time I had known her, I had never seen her with anyone and I realised there was a possibility she had never been involved with anyone since. It made me sad to think she had allowed that man to ruin her entire life, and it hardened me, made me determined not to allow Cara to do the same to me.

I was done crying and shaking and vomiting. I was done with Cara abusing me and controlling my life. I was done with being a victim.

It was the first night in too long that I did not bury my face in a pillow and cry myself to sleep.

I promised myself I would not allow Cara to win.

# CHAPTER ELEVEN

I felt a lot stronger in the morning. True to her word, Jasmine cooked me breakfast. Bacon, sausages, beans, eggs and a whole heap of hash browns. She made me double what she made herself, which, she said, was to make up for the fact I had hardly touched any food in the last couple of days. I did not complain and ate everything she gave me. She even offered me one of her own sausages, but I couldn't bring myself to take it.

"I'm not going to lie to you," she said while we ate, "your father's worried."

"I know. And I feel bad for that. I'll tell him when I get home tonight."

"You will?"

"I'm not sure. At the moment, yes, but I may chicken out."

"Want me to come with you?"

"No. No, I can't keep having everyone hold my hand all the time. Did he say anything?"

"About you? Sure. Plenty. He asked me what was wrong and I said it wasn't my place to tell him, which was true. He then asked me whether I thought it was as bad as you're making it out to be."

"What did you say to that?"

"I said sure it is. Anything that affects Ro this badly has to be bad, otherwise it wouldn't affect her.

## The Captain's Bombshell

He asked me whether I personally thought it was bad. And I again told him it wasn't my place to say."

"Poor man."

"Yeah, I thought that, too. So I threw him a bone and hoped you wouldn't mind. I told him it wasn't anything you couldn't get over, and that I'd help you get over it as soon as humanly possible. That seemed to make him happy. No idea why."

"He trusts you."

"He trusts you, too. That's why he's letting you do this."

We talked a little more, but there was work to be done so we could not sit and chat all morning. It was a shame, because it was peaceful sitting there with Jasmine. In her house, I had no worries.

We left the house together, but went our separate ways. Jasmine had told me nothing of her plans for the morning, but she needed me to keep the shop running while she did whatever it was she needed to do. It was the least I could do for her. Trade wasn't even too bad that morning. With my having broken some of the stock, we had room for everything we had intended to throw away. The sale on the trinkets did well and I even managed to shift a few postcards. The sun shone gloriously, which increased our trade in beach items, although my heart sank a little when I noticed a new delivery of green sandals had arrived.

Jasmine appeared at the shop shortly before midday and looked very pleased with herself.

"What?" I asked, her good humour infectious. "Jas, what have you done?"

"Stopped moping, for one thing. Last night, Ro, that was the first time I'd told anyone about what happened to me. I didn't do it for me, I did it for you. To be honest, I stopped caring about me a long time ago. But I shouldn't have."

"Jas?"

"Sorry, going off on one. My acting skills, that's what I'm talking about. I used my acting skills."

"You went for an audition this morning?" I asked with a frown, wanting to be happy for her but disappointed because I had thought she had an idea on how to help me. Then I felt bad for my selfishness all over again.

"No," she said. "Those postcards? I talked to the suppliers and traced them back to the printers. After all, Cara sold them to someone, so there has to be an audit trail somewhere. I went to the printers, turned up on their doorstep and demanded to see the manager. When he turned up, I threw a hissy fit and demanded to see *his* manager. I dug deep, used all the skills I ever learned all those years ago in acting school, dropped Cara's name a lot and finally got it."

"Got what?" I asked, her excitement overwhelming me.

"An address."

"For Cara?"

"No, for the people who created the image. We sell what the suppliers supply; the suppliers deliver what the printers print; the printers print what creators create. I have an address for the people who made the image. Those are the people who must have bought the picture from Cara."

"Then all we have to do is call them and tell them I didn't consent to my image being used, and they'll stop making them?"

"Call them?" She pulled a face. "If you want to get anywhere in this world, Ro, you have to kick up a stink. Threaten to sue them, march around them, shout as much as you can. And the only way you can properly do that is in person."

"You're going over there?"

"No. *We're* going over there."

"Tonight?"

"Right now."

"But ... but what about the shop?"

"The shop's had it, Ro."

"We've sold some postcards today and the sale's doing well. We can still save the shop, Jas."

"I don't care about the shop. Let the bank chase me for the money I owe them, it's only money. This is important. This is life-destroying stuff we're dealing with here and I'll be damned if I let you turn into me."

Her face fell slightly as she said this, as though she had not meant to say it. I felt bad for her all over again.

"If I end up half the woman you are," I said, "I'll be happy."

"I meant alone, miserable and pretending you're happy all the time."

"You mean you're not?"

"You're the one who tells me I'm a wonderful actress. But it won't happen to you, Ro. I'm not going to allow it to, and I have an address so we can make sure it won't. Grab your jacket, it's going to be chillier where we're going."

I did as I was told and helped Jasmine pull the shutter down on the shop. We hurried to her car and she drove for over an hour. I did not recognise the roads we were taking, for we had left Glazton behind some time earlier. Having such an intense love of the sea, I had never been far from Glazton and it was a new experience for me. Living by the seaside, there was simply nowhere I had ever wanted to take a holiday.

The town – perhaps even city – we had driven to was packed with cars and crowded with tall grey buildings. I imagined we had driven all the way to London, although even I knew London was not an hour's drive from Glazton. Jasmine pulled in to a parking space and we got out to feed the meter. Looking about, I was in awe of the strange place, for it was as far from Glazton as the sea was from a desert. There were people everywhere, so jammed onto the streets it was as though they were one immense wave. All the cars were honking their horns because no one was moving, or else were cutting ahead of one another and honking their horns anyway. No one, pedestrian or motorist, was stopping for red lights, which caused even more horns to be honked, while the ugly buildings overlooked it all, with scaffolding forming arches over the pavement as though they were metal braces for the teeth of the metropolis.

"You done staring?" Jasmine asked.

"Sorry. This is all new to me."

"You've never visited your friends in London?"

"No."

"No wonder Cara was able to trick you." She did not mean it in a nasty way and I did not take it as such. Cara's name no longer made me weak, for it was the name of my enemy and if I was going to fight her, it would have to make me strong.

Jasmine led me into a side-street, where the crowds were not so packed, and we approached a building of glass and grey stone. There was no sign over the door, which I had expected, although as we entered, I saw there were several company logos on the wall behind the reception desk. It must have meant there were several businesses operating out of the one building. Behind the reception desk was a lift lobby with what appeared to be six lifts in use.

It was all beyond anything I had ever seen before.

The receptionist smiled at us as we approached. "How can I help?" she asked.

Jasmine narrowed her eyes and said, "I want to speak with the manager of Charm Pictures."

The receptionist continued to smile as she punched something into her computer. I noted she wore a headset so would not need to use the telephone. "Can I ask whether you have an appointment?"

"You can ask whatever you like," Jasmine said. "I'm going to speak with the manager and I'm going to speak with him now."

"One moment." The receptionist spoke into her headpiece. It was clear the person she was speaking to was not the manager, but the receptionist likely worked for the building and not the company, so she would not impede our progress. Once she was done, she got us to fill in our names for our temporary badges and asked us to take the lift to the third floor.

Jasmine thanked her bluntly and we waited in the lobby. I was nervous but Jasmine was furious. She was getting into character and all over again I was astounded by her acting ability.

The lift came and we took it to the third floor, as requested. It opened into another lobby which ended in a locked door, accessible via key-card only. A man was waiting for us. He was not wearing a suit but did not look scruffy and I assumed we had arrived at an office of some form.

"You're not the manager, I take it," Jasmine said.

"No. Mr Tyler is a busy man. My name's Matthew. We can step into my office and discuss the problem you have."

"Why would I want to step into your office?" Jasmine asked. "I either speak with Mr Tyler or I go to the police."

"The police?"

"I'm here as a courtesy."

"If you're accusing this company of doing anything illegal, we'll have to consult our lawyers, but first we'll have to know what it is we've done."

"Do you recognise this young lady?"

He glanced at me. "No. Should I?"

"Should I? Should I? Are you trying to bury your company? Mr Tyler," she said, stepping so close to him their noses almost touched. "Now."

Matthew broke eye contact and cleared his throat. "This way, please," he said and walked to the door before swiping his pass and opening it. We walked into an open-plan office with dozens of tables and around forty members of staff. There was a lot of noise as people discussed their work or laughed about what had been on TV the previous night. Upon the walls were photographs and paintings, probably from various images they had created, while garish displays of employee of the month were pinned somewhat pointlessly to a display board.

Matthew attempted to get us into an office, but Jasmine scanned the room and made a firm decision of who the manager was. For my part, I had no idea, but Jasmine clearly had this all worked out.

"Mr Tyler," she said, storming through the office towards a man in his fifties. All eyes turned upon us and, while the talking continued, it was mainly whispering now. The man Jasmine had focused upon looked terrified as she approached his desk and scowled at him. "I would advise you call your lawyers, Mr Tyler. You're going to need them."

"I don't think he has any lawyers," a man behind another desk said. He was aged somewhere in his forties, wore a suit with neither tie nor top button, and looked the smarmiest individual I had ever seen. "I'm Mr Tyler."

Jasmine abandoned her attack upon the man she had selected and strolled over to Tyler's desk. He leaned back in his chair, played with a pencil and did not look at all bothered.

"What can I do for you?" he asked. "Miss …?"

"Ms Chakma."

"Ms. One of those."

"Do you recognise my companion?"

Tyler looked over at me and winked. "Nope. Even if I was drunk, I would have remembered that one."

There were a few chuckles about the office.

"Please continue," Jasmine said sharply. "It'll look great when it comes to court. Mr Tyler, I'm Miss

Shelby's lawyer. I'm building a case against you and wanted to hear your side of things."

That lost him some of his smirk but he attempted to regain it for the sake of his image. "Let's find an office to discuss this."

"Let's discuss it here," Jasmine said. "Does anyone in this office recognise Miss Shelby?"

No one wanted to meet her gaze and everyone pretended to be busy. Jasmine waited in silence until someone decided she was going to stand there forever and said, "Bombshell."

"What was that?" Jasmine asked.

"The Captain's Bombshell," a woman said, sounding nervous. "That's who she is, right?"

"That's what you called her, yes," Jasmine said. "I'm not going to beat around the bush, Mr Tyler. My client had some candid photographs taken by her boyfriend. Those photos were stolen by one Ms Cara Hughes and sold to this company, who then illegally turned one of those images into a series of postcards."

"Now hold on," Tyler said. "We bought ..."

"You didn't check the validity of your source," Jasmine interrupted. "Ms Hughes had no right to sell you those photos because she stole them from the copyright holder. You've printed stolen property, violated copyright and displayed candid, sexy images of a young woman without her permission. Your failure to vet your sources has just landed you an incredibly expensive lawsuit, Mr Tyler. If I were you, I would stop trying to look flash in front of your staff and assess what you can possibly to do make amends."

"We'll stop distribution of the postcards, of course," he said. "Tina, stop distribution of the postcards."

"That's not good enough," Jasmine said. "How many pictures did you buy off Ms Hughes?"

"Twenty. We've only used the one so far, but we're spreading them out over the course of ..."

"So far?"

"I mean, we only got around to using one."

"Halt production of the others, obviously. And transfer copies of all the images to my legal team." She handed him a card, which was foresight I had not expected. It would not get us the originals, but at least we would know which pictures Tyler had of me.

"Tina, get copies of those photos," Tyler said, trying to maintain a sense of control even though he was falling apart under Jasmine's assault.

"There will of course be a full investigation," she said without missing a beat. "If you've acquired pictures of one woman through illegal means, who's to say there won't be more? I've personally been reviewing some of the other images you've been using in your various projects and it doesn't look good for you."

"Tina, put a note in my calendar for me to do a full audit."

"I've spoken to a few of the women in question," Jasmine continued, "and one of them was very interesting. She had no idea you were using her image to promote your line of racy postcards; the first she knew of it was when I turned up on her doorstep. Of course, legally I could only speak to her with her parents present, because she's a minor."

Tyler's face lost all colour then and he said, "Tina ..."

"Tina," Jasmine cut him off, "clear Mr Tyler's schedule for the foreseeable future. He's going to be a very busy man. And, if you haven't done so already, get onto his lawyers."

Behind Jasmine, I was keeping quiet. I had never seen her like this, for she was fired up with so much passion I totally believed everything she was saying. I knew the part about her being a lawyer was a lie, of course, but she had me half convinced she had indeed been round to see all these other women. I wondered whether any other women even existed.

"Which brings us onto Ms Hughes," Jasmine said. "I assume you have contact details for her?"

"Yes, yes, I ..." He looked to Tina but did not have the courage to ask her anything.

"Tina," Jasmine said, "would you please get me Ms Hughes's contact details?"

Tina did this very quickly and printed them off. Jasmine glanced at the page and folded it before placing it into her inside pocket.

"Someone from my office will get in touch with her," Jasmine said, "and I'll personally be in contact with you, Mr Tyler. For your sake, I would advise you to have no communication with her at all. Anything you say to her from this moment on will legally compromise you. Right now, I have a gut feeling you didn't know the photos were illegal. But the law doesn't operate on gut feelings."

"I won't talk to her," Tyler promised.

"And make Tina a coffee once in a while. She deserves it."

He rose from his desk.

"Not right this second," Jasmine said.

He sat back down.

"All right, we're done," Jasmine said. "You can make her that coffee now."

He rose and hastened over to the kitchen area as Jasmine and I strode back across the office. Everyone was looking at her but no one dared to speak a word. We got into the lift and rode it down to the ground floor, where we left the building and returned to the car. It was not until we were safely inside the vehicle that Jasmine exhaled and I could see she was shaking.

"How did I do?" she asked.

"That was ... I ... You were amazing."

I threw myself at her and enveloped her in a fierce hug. I could feel the tension flood from her.

"Thanks," she said. "I was nervous as hell in there."

"You didn't show it. You're the best actress I've ever seen."

That pleased her and she produced the paper from her pocket. She handed it to me. Upon it were printed Cara's home address and phone number. I stared at the page, a mixture of emotions surging through me. Elation, fear, relief ... so many others I could not name.

"You OK?" Jasmine asked. "This is what we wanted, right?"

"I know, I ... Do you know, in all the time I was with Cara, all I wanted was her number? She was evasive about it, and whenever I remembered to ask for it again, it was too late. This is what I wanted before, but for different reasons. Back then, I thought gaining her number would put me onto a path to live my dream."

"And now?"

"Now? Now having her number will allow me to end the nightmare."

"You really do have a way with words, Ro," Jasmine said as she pulled away from the kerb.

Settling back in my seat, I was glad of what we had achieved, yet at the same time I was worried. I had not spoken with Cara since the photoshoot and there was a chance she was not the villain at all. There was a chance she had been deceived just as I had been. I did not believe it, for even my heart was telling me I was the gullible naïve fool everyone else had seen before. I wanted to believe in Cara, yet I didn't.

I supposed I would find out one way or another once we met.

For the entire journey, I sat silently with my thoughts and fears, knowing that soon I would face Cara again.

# CHAPTER TWELVE

Cara lived in a town about an hour away, although I knew so little of British geography that I did not know which direction we had taken. We could have been two hours from Glazton, we could have been ten minutes, and I would not have known. It was neither the pleasant free town of Glazton, nor the cold industrial grey of where we had just departed. There were green areas, with trees lining the roads, but mainly there were houses. Jasmine pulled the car into an estate where high-rising flats stretched to the heavens. We got out of the car and found the air cold, for we were used to the heat of Glazton. There was rubbish spread out across the field beside us and children played with a ball. Some youths were hanging around with their bicycles, while a woman lay on her back while working on the undercarriage of her car.

"This certainly isn't Glazton," Jasmine said.

"Jas, I'd like you to wait in the car."

"Are you joking with me?"

"This is something I have to do by myself."

"Ro, you need me for moral support. Maybe even to restrain you if you decide to pummel her face in."

"I'm not a violent person, Jas."

"What if she attacks you, then?"

"You're my backup to make sure she doesn't do that."

"Ro, I get what you're doing, but you shouldn't be alone right now. Especially not with her."

"Cara won't hurt me. Not physically anyway. I can't believe everything she said, everything she was, was a lie."

"Please tell me you're not still in love with her."

"I didn't know her long enough to fall in love. Maybe I thought I was – actually, yes, I did think I was – but I wasn't. I know that. I just need to face her, Jas, and get her to be honest with me. And I have to do that alone."

Jasmine looked around while she considered, then nodded. "I don't like this and I don't agree with it, but I understand. Call me the instant something goes wrong. Don't call the police, call me and I'll call the police."

"Thank you, Jasmine. You're a good friend."

I could see she wanted to say something, to offer some further support, but there was nothing really she could say. "If you're not back in an hour," she finally went with, "I'm calling the police anyway."

I smiled, but it was tight and full of fear. For a moment, I thought she might hug me, but she was too scared even to do that. Instead, she hung around her car and watched me approach the estate.

As I walked into the shadow of the great building, I grew even colder and wished I had brought a warmer jacket. There were graffiti on the walls, but nothing fancy and there was evidence there had been attempts to scrub the walls clean. I tried the door, not knowing whether it was going to be locked, but it opened easily and I could see the lock was broken anyway. I had memorised Cara's address and worked my way slowly up the concrete stairs until I reached the right level. Walking along the stone corridor, I looked down to see Jasmine waiting impatiently by the car. Her arms were folded and she was pacing, which was never a good sign with her. I had brought her into my mess and promised myself I would make it up to her once it was all done. I would find the money to replace the glass statues I had broken, I would organise funding for her shop and I would save her business. I had no idea how, but I would make it up to her and she would be happy again.

I had visions of finding that fake director and giving him a good firm kick between the legs, but that was never going to happen. He was long gone; he had ruined Jasmine's life and had long ago forgotten all about her. Even if I somehow did catch up to him, I imagined I would have to run through all the details of his crime just to make him remember.

Arriving at Cara's door, I stopped and composed myself. Confronting Cara was the most harrowing thing I had ever done and the longer I stood there, the more chance there was of me running away. I had felt something for her, something magical. Perhaps it had not been love, but it had certainly been a strong contender for it. But what had she felt for me? Loathing? Affection? Boredom? Had she felt anything at all?

The only way for me to know would be to knock on her door. Raising my hand, I rapped lightly and stepped back, taking deep breaths to steady myself.

No one answered, so I approached the door again and gave it a hard, solid thump.

"All right, all right," someone shouted from within. "No need to break my door down."

The door opened and Cara stood there, wearing dark trousers and a loose white vest. There was anger in her eyes, although as she saw me her expression changed. She was confused, perhaps a little scared, although all this passed in a moment and her face soured.

"What?" she asked.

"Do you even recognise me?"

"Not with your clothes on, no."

"Can I come in?"

"What do you want to come in for?"

"To talk."

"Why would you want to talk to me?"

"Because we need to talk."

"Rowena, go home. You're a swell kid, but I have stuff to do."

She slammed the door in my face.

I blinked, uncertain that had just happened. I was not tearful, I had long moved beyond that stage. I was not even furious, for I refused to allow Cara to get under my skin. I thumped on her door again. This time, she ignored me.

The door beside hers opened and a burly man stepped out. He had a beer gut which threatened to split his shirt further than it already was and for some reason he wasn't wearing any trousers, just an old, worn pair of underpants. Up both arms were tattoos and his eyes were bleary, either from having just been woken or from far too many drugs.

"Keep the noise down," he growled.

"Mind your own business." I thumped again.

"Hey, I'm talking to you," he said. The door to Cara's other side opened then and a gaunt woman in her fifties emerged. Her skin had yellowed through too much tobacco and she swore at the dogs barking about her legs.

"What's going on out here?" she asked, only with a lot of expletives.

"I'm trying to talk to Cara," I said, thumping the door again. "Cara! Open the door!"

"She doesn't want to talk to you," the man said. "You a bailiff?"

"Do I look like a bailiff? Cara!"

"You from the bank?" the woman asked.

"No. Cara! You can't just kiss me the way you did and leave me hanging. You take me back to your place, get me naked and then don't want to talk again? That's not how relationships work!"

The man took a step back. "What are you on, girl?"

I had experienced my fair share of discrimination over the years and had a feeling Cara would not want her dirty laundry aired in a public place. I thumped again, louder than ever. "Cara! Open the door! Are you even a lesbian?"

The door opened, Cara grabbed me and hauled me in. I released a startled meep as she slammed it closed again.

"What the hell are you doing?" she snarled now that we were alone in the flat.

"Giving you a small taste of what ruining your life is like."

"I didn't ruin your life."

"You heartless ... You have no idea what you've done."

"I took some photos you posed for. *You* posed for. I didn't force you to do anything."

"You lied to me."

"I lie to everyone."

"Why?"

"Why what?"

"Why did you do it?"

"Ro, I don't have time for this. You had a crush on me. Get over it. I have."

"Did you feel anything at all?"

"Oh God, you're still whinging about it, aren't you?"

I laughed. The sound was strained. "No. I'm not hung up on you, Cara. I just wanted to know whether any of it was true."

"Any of what? What I felt? No, I didn't love you. But you loved me and I took a little payment for that. I showed you a fun time and I got paid for it."

"Well, that makes you a certain kind of woman, doesn't it?"

"I whore my soul, yes. Never claimed otherwise. Now get out."

"No."

"You want me to officially dump you? Consider yourself officially dumped. Now get out."

"No."

"Shame you didn't say that word often enough when we were together."

Cara was making it very difficult not to hate her. She was by the front door, which allowed me to turn around and march into her living-room. It was as small as the studio and it was an absolute tip. Papers were strewn everywhere, packaging and spare parts for her cameras littered the floor. The carpet was thin and threadbare in places, the edges frayed by mice which had scratched it away for their nests. The walls were painted a dull green and there were large cracks in them, with black damp staining the ceiling. The only item of furniture in the whole room was a broken table, supported by books but still wonky. There were no pictures hanging on the walls, nor ornaments denoting any character. Empty crisp packets and biscuit wrappers lay all about, as though this was all she ever ate.

I instantly felt sorry for her, but brushed aside such sympathy because she didn't deserve it.

"At least I've discovered one thing," I said, glancing to the painted walls. "I know why you don't like green: it reminds you of home."

"Get out."

"No."

She stood before me, furious, but short of physically attacking me there was little she could do. The very thought that she was powerless gave me strength.

"This is your life," I said. "This is your sorry little life, Cara. No wonder you ran away for a seaside romance."

"What do you want?" she asked angrily. "An apology? A cut of my profits? I don't have any profits, Rowena. I don't have any money."

"You don't have any furniture, either."

"Everything's gone. The debt collectors came and took everything. You don't even want to know how much I owe. Yes, I took advantage of you, yes I took photos of you and sold them to whoever would buy them. There's nothing you can do about it. Sue me. Oh, wait, I don't have any money."

"How many other girls have you preyed on?"

"None. You were an easy target, Ro. I mean look at you. You're young, pretty, you have an all-over tan and bouncing red hair to die for. You were made to be in front of the camera. You were made for people like me to take advantage of. That's what life's all about – taking advantage of people. Everyone wants something, Ro, and everyone has a price. A guy chats me up in a bar? He wants to get his leg over, so I let him buy me a drink or two before I tell him to get lost. That's a woman's prerogative. You use what you have and if you use it properly, you succeed."

"That's a heartless view of life."

She laughed. "You have no idea, do you? How could you? You're perfection. You think people smile at you because they're being friendly? You think people chat to you at a bus stop because they're bored? You think someone opens a door for you because it's polite? Pretty girls don't understand real life, Rowena. You get what you want out of people because those people are conditioned to bend over backwards for pretty girls. I've had to fight for everything in life, I've had to struggle just to be noticed. Everything falls in your lap, Rowena, so yeah I used you."

"You're jealous? You did all that to me because you're jealous?"

"I'm not jealous," she shouted. "I'm angry. Angry at a society which gives girls like you everything."

"Girls like me? Cara, you have no idea, do you?"

"What?"

"How old are you? I never asked, but I always figured you were thirty."

"I am thirty. Why?"

"Because you're eight years older than me and I thrilled at being with you. You say you had a hard life because you're not the perfection of beauty? I don't think you understand what beauty is. It's not what a person looks like, Cara. It's what a person is."

"Don't you dare shove that moralistic twaddle onto me."

"Beauty is a smile, the twinkle of the eyes, the tilt of the head. Beauty is being able to listen, being able to laugh. Beauty is understanding and acceptance. While you were pretending to like me, Cara, you were beautiful. You don't get that. I didn't care that you were older, I didn't care what you looked like. I only cared what I felt about you, and you don't deserve to know how deeply I did feel."

That took some of the anger from her. She was confused by my words and again I had to force myself not to feel sorry for her.

"Cara," I asked, "are you a lesbian?"

"No."

"You kiss girls pretty well for someone who isn't a lesbian."

"I do whatever I have to for money. And, for your information, that kiss we shared on the beach made me sick."

"That kiss we shared lasted almost an hour."

"It did?" She shook her head. "I'm not getting into this with you. You're not converting me, Rowena."

"Converting you? Sexuality isn't a religion. And I'm not flirting with you. I wouldn't take you back even if you dropped at my feet and begged. I'm just trying to explain to you how close you came to happiness. For just a couple of days, you put aside the monster you are and pretended to be someone good and decent. If you could do that again, you might actually be happy. Instead, you live in this squalor, with people chasing you for money and no one to turn to for help."

Cara looked away. She perched on the edge of her wonky table. "Just tell me what you want and get out of my life."

"I want to be happy. I want to find a nice girl to spend time with. I want to picnic on the beach and share biscuits and Curly Wurlies. I want to kiss in the heat of the sun and taste chocolate on her tongue. I want to lie naked in my special, secluded place where my girlfriend and I can get an all-over tan without anyone seeing us. I want to spend the day on the beach and the evening on the pier. I want to work hard during the day and come home at night to curl up on the settee with someone I love. I want to grow more in love with that special girl every single day that passes."

"I meant what do you want from me?"

I stared at her long and hard. "None of that, Cara. I don't want anything more to do with you. You're a parasite. I've tried to feel sorry for you, I've tried to justify what you did to me. I've tried my best to understand you, but you're just a bitter and twisted woman who couldn't hang a mirror in her flat because she wouldn't be able to stand the sight of herself."

"Are you done?"

"No. I want the photos you took of me."

"I don't have them."

"Of course you have them. The nude ones. I want to know who you sold them to."

"Good luck with that."

"So you did sell them?"

"Of course I sold them. They were gold from a mine."

If I had received such confirmation only a day earlier, I would have collapsed in a shivering heap; but that was no longer who I was. "I'm going to find the name of the company," I said, "and I'm going to phone the police on them. They've illegally acquired naked pictures of me and when I sue them, they're coming after you. If you think you're in debt now, you have no idea."

"Don't threaten me in my own home."

"This isn't a home, Cara. It's where you've come to die." I looked around and moved over to her camera equipment.

"Hey, what are you doing?"

The first camera I picked up was digital – most of her cameras were – and I turned it on and cycled through the pictures she had taken. They were mostly scenic shots and none of the beach, so I put it down and tried the next one.

"You can't go through my stuff like this," she said.

"You haven't tried to stop me, which means you know if you lay a finger on me, I'm calling the police."

She took a step back and ran her hands through her spiky hair. She reminded me of when I had initially refused to pose for her, when she had acted as though I had ruined things for her. I could tell she was not acting this time.

The second camera revealed nothing, either, although the third had some pictures of the beach. There were none of me, though.

That was when I noticed her laptop poking out from behind a stack of papers. Picking it up made Cara start for me, but I held her back with a glower. The laptop was already on and I clicked onto her picture folder. There was one labelled 'Ro' and I opened it to find so many photos that the computer was taking its time in loading them all. The counter at the bottom said there were four hundred and fifty-seven of them in total. As they loaded, I was greeted with not only the images of me in my swimsuit, but also of the disgraceful shots of my nude body. Cara had taken so many in such a rapid-fire sequence, I could have run through them all quickly and watched me do a striptease with an image quality as great as any video she might have taken.

"Give me a couple of memory sticks," I said.

"Why? They all fit on just one."

"You've made copies?"

She bit her lip and narrowed her eyes. I sifted through the papers and found a stack of flash drives. Inserting the first into the laptop, I discovered it contained nothing of interest to me. Cara said nothing while I tried each in turn. I eventually found all the pictures of me on a single memory stick. The total number on the drive matched those on the laptop. Pocketing the drive, I selected all the files on her computer and deleted them. It did not take the computer long to do so and I opened the recycle bin in order to destroy them properly.

"What's it worth not to do that?" Cara asked as my finger poised above the enter button.

"What's it worth? Cara, you don't have any money."

"I can do something else, anything else." Her eyes were frantic. "Come on, Ro, you can't do this to me."

"I won't delete the pictures," I said, "if you tell me the name of the company you sold the nude photos to."

"Yes, yes. Hold on." She rooted through the paperwork until she found the one she wanted. "Here." She handed it across to me. It was an invoice for a company called Greyliant Publishing. There was an address on the invoice and an amount that startled me.

"They paid how much?"

"Yeah," Cara said. "Like I said, you're a gold-mine. You delete those photos, Ro, and you're throwing away a fortune. All right, I shouldn't have sold the photos without your permission, but I was desperate. Wet Daydreams, that's the name of the magazine Greyliant's publishing your photos in."

"How many did you sell them?"

"Check the invoice."

I did. She had sold them twenty-seven pictures in total.

"Ro, listen to me. We can work together on this. They already want you to pose for some more. Full nudity this time, obviously, but they want other outfits, other scenes. They have a beach theme, right? Wet Daydreams. They want shots of you in the sea, lying naked on the surf, building sandcastles, dripping ice cream down you. Come on, Ro, it'll be fun. What do you say?"

I looked into her hopeful eyes and said, "You honestly expect me to consider what you're asking?"

"Ro, come on. I ... no!"

I hit the button and watched as the photos were emptied from the recycle bin.

"Oh, you stupid ... I can't believe you just ... Ugh!" she stormed across the room and kicked something. I thought I would have felt good about what I had done, I thought I would have a great weight lifted from my shoulders. Instead, I just felt numb. It was a sensation I was coming to understand quite well of late.

"You know," I said, "I'm glad I came. Not just so I could delete the photos, but because I finally get to see you for who you are, Cara. I thought I was in love with you. I'm not going to pretend otherwise, I genuinely thought I was in love with you. But looking at you now makes me sick. And to think of what I put myself through, to think of what I did after you left me ..." I shook my head.

"Ro, wait. Please just leave it. If you cause trouble, they'll come after me. They'll want their money back but it's already gone. The debt collectors came round yesterday. They took everything that wasn't nailed down. The money's gone. If you do this to me, I won't be able to repay them. I won't be able to do anything."

"I don't think you understand something, Cara. I don't care." Setting down her laptop, I was about to leave when I caught sight of something in the corner of the room. Moving over to it, I picked it up in astonishment. "The swimsuit," I said. "You kept it?" I also found the cap and the discovery confused me.

"Why would I throw it away?" she asked. "It was a memento, Ro. It was my final memory of our time together. It smells of you, it reminds me of you every time I'm down."

"It sure does smell of me," I said. "I seem to recall sweating like a pig. Have you even washed it?"

"I meant to, but my water was cut off."

"Why would you keep this? God, you haven't been wearing it, have you?"

"No. I just couldn't bear to part with it."

The swimsuit provided a spark of hope that there was still some good in Cara, that for even a fleeting moment my affection had meant something to her. Then my heart glazed over as I realised the true reason she had kept it.

"You were going to use it again," I said. "You were going to con some other poor sap into posing for you."

"No, I was keeping it because it reminded me of you."

"Were you even going to wash it first?"

She looked at me sourly. "All right, yes, I was going to con someone else into wearing it. Happy now?"

"You're pathetic. And I'm taking the costume."

"That's mine."

"The costume's yours, the sweat is mine. I'd say I own at least half of it."

"Your logic is screwy."

"So are your morals." I stormed off towards the door and stopped as I opened it. "I didn't know what to expect when I came here, Cara. I wanted to believe you cared for me, I wanted to believe you'd been forced to sell the photos, that you were avoiding me because you were ashamed. I wanted to think you could have loved me. But you're incapable of love. You're like a junkie who can only focus on her next fix. I hope you find someone to love, Cara, and for your sake I hope they don't use you like you used me."

"You have no idea what you're doing to me."

"You know what? I've had it with you. I can't believe I jumped off the pier over you."

Her mouth opened to shout abuse, but she stopped. "You what?"

I had not meant to say that, but I was so angry I no longer cared about anything. "Yes," I said. "I was so ashamed, so violated by what you did to me that I tried to kill myself. Thank heaven for the lifeguards, Cara. Thank heaven the lifeguards don't have the same attitude as you when it comes to saving people who just want to die."

"Ro, I ... I never meant to push you that far."

"You know what, Cara? Save it. I don't care." I walked out of her flat and almost collided with the tattooed man and the gaunt woman, who were both eavesdropping at the door. They stepped aside to let me through. The woman looked angry and the burly man gave me a respectful nod. I continued walking, my head held high, and returned to where Jasmine was waiting.

She was leaning against her car, arms folded, although she straightened as she saw me approach. "How'd it go?" she asked.

"Well enough."

"Did you get what you wanted?"

"Her pictures are gone and I have copies in my back pocket. I also picked up a little something else."

"I noticed. That's the swimsuit you wore, right?"

I nodded.

"Why do you want it?"

"I don't," I said. "I just don't want Cara to have it. I don't want her to have anything of mine."

Jasmine glanced up to the flats above and said, "Let's get out of here, Ro. This place is making me feel ill."

Shoving the swimsuit onto the back seat, I got back into the passenger side and buckled myself in as Jasmine pulled the car out. We drove from Cara's home and I knew I would never see her again.

The numbness was at last beginning to lift, for I could feel again. And what I felt was warmth that I was discarding everything that did not matter and that I was keeping close to me the people who truly loved me and whom I could love in return.

# CHAPTER THIRTEEN

It was a relief to return to Glazton. Jasmine parked the car close to the shop but made no move to open up for business. Instead, she bought us some fish and chips from the place next door and we sat on the beach and ate. It was around half three and we were both starving, for we had eaten nothing since breakfast. For the first time in ages, I had no sandwiches from my father, but the fish was divine. I even removed my T-shirt and trousers so I could soak up the sun. It had been a part of my routine for so long that it was something I did not want to get out of.

"It makes me happy to see you haven't changed for her," Jasmine said. She was sitting on the sand with her legs beneath her, while I was lying beside her propped up on my elbow. The fish and chips lay between us, spread out on paper. Needless to say, we kept a careful watch for seagulls.

"I won't change anything," I said. "I'm a little wiser now, hopefully less naïve. The next time a pretty girl comes my way, I'm going to keep my head."

"Love does strange things to people."

"Have you ever been in love, Jas?"

She tensed.

"Sorry," I said.

"You don't have to be sorry," she said, forcing a smile. "I've never had time for love, I've always been too busy."

"Yet you closed up the shop to help me."

"I should say I like to keep myself busy. It stops me having to face reality."

I considered that. "Do you know, in all the time I've known you, I've never seen you on the beach."

"I've been on the beach plenty of times, Ro."

"I meant sunbathing. Look at me, I'm lying here in a bikini. You're wearing a shirt and trousers."

"I'm not wearing a bikini under this. I can't just strip off."

"You sell bikinis, Jas. The shop's just over there; if you wanted one, you could just go get one. No one else is buying them anyway."

"I don't feel comfortable wearing that sort of thing. I look at you sometimes and imagine what I would have been like at your age. You're at a special time of your life, Ro. You're young enough to enjoy yourself but old enough to know what you're doing."

"A little cryptic but I think I know what you're trying to say. Jas, you're thirty-one. You're not old."

"Old enough."

"You're spending so much time helping me, I want to do something for you."

"I don't need you to do anything for me. I'm perfectly happy as I am."

"You're miserable and just act happy. You said as much yourself."

"Did I? I didn't mean to."

"Jas, I'm making it my mission to bring you back to life."

"Excuse me?"

"You lack self-confidence, that's all. You're as pretty as I am and you're not an old prune yet. When I've destroyed those nude photos, I'm making it my mission to get you on the beach in a bikini."

"There's something twisted about that sentence, Ro."

"The difference is I don't want those photos to exist, but you do want to be here in a bikini."

"What makes you say that?"

"Because you look uncomfortable."

"And how does that mean I want to sit here half naked?"

"Because you care too much about me. And if you care enough to be with me when I've been saved from attempted suicide, it means you're a loving person. And loving people don't want to spend their lives alone."

"I don't need a man in my life to make me happy."

"Hey, that's my motto."

She chuckled at that.

"That's a good sound," I said.

"Sounds like something your father would say."

"Actually, it was. Say, Dad's single. You get on well with him, right?"

"Ro, your father's over ten years older than me."

"What's in a few years?"

"Didn't you think that about Cara?"

"Are you comparing my father to Cara?"

"What? No. Your dad's a kind, sweet generous man who brought you into my life."

I sighed heavily. "Sounds like love to me."

"Would you stop already?" Her dark cheeks were turning red and I stopped teasing in horror.

"Hold on a ..." I said. "No, wait a minute. You can't think like that about Dad. He's my dad."

"I don't think like that about anyone. You were the one who said it."

"And you're the one who's blushing."

"I'm not blushing."

"Jas, my dad. Really? Eew."

"Ro, stop it."

I looked out to sea, wishing I had never started the jibes at all. Yet the more I thought about it, the more I found I didn't mind. Then I laughed aloud at the possibility and tried to think of all the times Jasmine and my father had talked and whether there had been any electricity between them. I imagined how they would ask each other out, not realising they were both interested, how they would step on each other's feet while they danced, how they would disappear all night and I would be phoning them to ask what they thought they were getting up to.

"Ro, you can stop daydreaming," she said sternly.

"Sorry, it's what I do."

It was good to be merry again. It was good for things to be back to normal between us and for the world to be at rights.

"We're getting there, aren't we?" Jasmine asked after a while. "With the photos, I mean."

"I think so. It's strange to think I should have asked for help all along."

"Yeah, there's a lesson to be learned from all of this. I'll need the paperwork from Greyliant."

"Jas, I'm the one who needs to call them."

"You're not the one with the acting skills."

"You were Oscar-worthy back at that postcard place."

She tossed her hair and adopted an air of graceful smugness. "It's a talent."

Picking up my trousers, I pulled out the invoice I had taken from Cara. It had all the information we would need about Greyliant Publishing. As I pulled it, something else fell from my pocket. It was a folded-up piece of paper and I opened it, wondering what it was. Staring out at me was a scratchy, pencil-like image of two women smiling as their photograph was taken in a booth.

Jasmine sensed something was wrong and she glanced at it. "Bad memories."

"Good memories," I said. "Good memories of a bad person." I folded it back up and did not want to litter the beach so tucked it back into my trouser pocket. "I know this is all a mess, Jas, but Cara was fun to be with."

"Was she, though?"

"Sometimes. She was domineering, overpowering and obnoxious, but she looked me in the eyes when we were talking and she didn't dismiss *everything* I had to say."

"That sounds like a solid basis for a permanent relationship. Ro, you can't dwell on her. I know you like to see the good in everybody, and that's sweet, but right now it's you or her."

"What do you mean?"

"You know what I mean, even if you don't want to accept it. When I call this number, there's going to be a lot of trouble coming Cara's way. But if I don't call it, those pictures are going to come out and the trouble's going to find you instead. Either she suffers or you do, it's that simple."

I understood what she was saying and she was right in that I had already given the matter a lot of thought. "If she was someone I cared about," I said, "I wouldn't do it. If this was you or Dad or even Sophie, I'd tear up that invoice and suffer everything coming my way." I paused, glanced up as I heard a seagull pass by overhead, its eyes on our lunch. "But she's nothing to me, Jas. Just as I was nothing to her."

"You don't sound angry."

"I'm not. I think I was at some point, but I'm not angry with her. Cara did what was in her nature. And her nature was to be a deceptive, cold-hearted monster. That's not me. Which is why I've actually considered not contacting these people. It's not about her winning, Jas, it's about me losing. If we could both come out of this smelling of roses, I'd take that option."

"I know you would. And you know what that tells me?"

"That I'm still naïve?"

"That one day you're going to end up with someone wonderful. You're going to get married, buy a house overlooking the beach and adopt a few kids. You'll be the best wife ever, the best mother, the best woman to ever walk the earth. Because that's who you are, Rowena Shelby. You're caring and loving and if you could, you would hug the world until it cried with remorse for all the sins that had been committed upon it."

It was rare for Jasmine to show such emotion. At work, she was reserved, and she only ever seemed to get emotional when she was defending me. "Thank you," I said. "I think I needed that. I wish there was a gay version of you somewhere out there because I'd probably marry her."

"Could I have the invoice, please?"

I handed it over and Jasmine produced her mobile phone. She punched in the number and waited for it to ring. In the meantime, she put it on speakerphone so I could hear what was being said.

After three rings, it was picked up by a woman. "Good afternoon, Greyliant Publishing, Cathy speaking, how may I help you?"

"Hi, Cathy," Jasmine said. "I was after someone in charge of a magazine called Wet Daydreams. I don't have a name but anyone with any sort of authority would do."

"One moment, please." There was a pause. Then Cathy came back on. "I've spoken to Wet Daydreams and can put you through to their admin department. If you explain to them who you are and what you need, they can direct you."

"Thanks, Cathy."

The phone rang again while we were reconnected.

"So far, so good," I said.

Jasmine wrinkled her nose.

A male voice picked up. "Hi, this is Wet Daydreams."

"Jasmine Chakma. I need to speak with someone in charge."

"Can I ask what it's concerning?"

"A lawsuit being field against you for using illegal pictures."

Illegal pictures. That was clever of her. With magazines of that nature, there would be studious checks on the women used in their photos, and if there were accusations of illegal pictures, the assumption would be that the models were underage. The nameless man put us on hold for a minute or so before coming back on.

"Thanks for waiting," he said. "I'm putting you through to Eliza Yaren. She's our editor and she's agreed to speak with you directly over this."

"How gracious of her," Jasmine said.

The next voice to come on was that of a woman. She sounded tight, with a faint Japanese accent. She was cautious yet defensive. "This is Ms Yaren," she said. "You have something you'd like to report, Ms Chakma?"

"Ms Yaren, good afternoon."

"Good afternoon."

"I'm informed you use a freelance photographer by the name of Cara Hughes."

"If we do, I'm not at liberty to discuss such information, especially over the phone."

"Understandably," Jasmine said. "But I should tell you I have in my hand an invoice printed on office paperwork from Wet Daydreams of Greyliant Publishing. It's payment for photographs purchased by Ms Hughes. Quite a few photographs."

"Again, I couldn't possibly discuss the matter over the phone. Are you a solicitor perhaps?"

"No, I run a shop on the seafront."

I was surprised Jasmine was not still pretending to be my lawyer but she had clearly thought through how she was going to play this. Since we had done nothing wrong, she had opted to go with the truth, which would likely help us further down the line.

"Ms Hughes tricked the woman in those shots to pose for her and sold the images to you without permission. If you've printed them, you're in violation of her civil rights."

"I don't want to keep repeating myself, Ms Chakma, so I'm not going to mention the names of any freelancers who may or may not work for us; but, hypothetically speaking, if someone did sell us photographs of a model who did not consent to her images being used for publication, that would be a matter to be taken up between the artist and the model."

"Wow," I said. "I never knew sentences could even be that long."

"I didn't quite catch that," Yaren said.

"That was Rowena," Jasmine said. "She's the woman in the photos. She's not a model, just a young woman who trusted the wrong person. Not to mention your freelancers by name, but it seems at least one of them is in the habit of entrapping young women with promises of love, before exposing them in your magazines for all the world to see. If this artist, as you call her, has done it once, chances are she'll have done it before. If I went on-line and bought a load of back copies of your magazine, I think there's a possibility I could track down some of the women you've used and find they have a similar story."

"You couldn't possibly track down girls just from their photographs. We don't use their real names in the text."

"No. But we have the Internet today, Ms Yaren. We have social media and we have forums. If I put enough work in, I reckon I could find some other victims. Some may not even be aware their photos have been used. They may have just been sitting at home, leading the life of a recluse while they battled depression and the bottle over what Cara did to them. This could be a real eye-opener for you, Ms Yaren. Within six months, I think I might be able to flush out a dozen victims or more. And you say you don't use the real names of the women? That's true, but you do credit the name of the photographer. It'll give me a good start to know which women to track down."

I sincerely hoped that was true, for if Yaren did not credit the photographer, the entire conversation would be over.

There was a long pause on the other end but Yaren had not put us on hold; she was just thinking.

"Could you come to our office so we can discuss this in person?" Yaren asked.

"That depends where your office is."

"Wardour Street, Central London."

"London?" I asked. "That's miles away."

"Then don't bother," Yaren said snidely, "and stop wasting my time."

"Of course we'll come to London," Jasmine said. "What time does your office close?"

"Around six."

We would not get to London by six, and I could not imagine explaining to my father that Jasmine and I were driving all the way over there anyway.

"We'll arrive in the morning," Jasmine said. "That gives you an opportunity to prepare for our arrival."

"Good," Yaren said. "If you can convince us this girl you're with is the one in the photos, we'll consider pulling them from specials and not using any further pictures. There's nothing I can do about any which have already been published, of course."

"We'll take this as it comes," Jasmine said. "Thank you for your time." She hung up and put away her phone. "What did you think?"

"I think you're doing me more good than I ever did myself. What if they contact Cara?"

"They have all night, I'm sure they'll contact her. She'll probably ignore them, but even if they speak with her, they'll be able to hear from her nervousness that we're telling the truth. I suppose there's a chance she could convince them she's above-board, but Yaren's going to be checking into all the photos Cara's ever sold her. She may not have sounded like she was scared, but things like this will panic people in those jobs."

"Why?"

"Because they're supposed to verify their sources. Even if you take underage nudity out of the equation, there's still the matter of consent. The way the world is nowadays, consent is paramount."

"What about the shop? You can't afford to keep it closed for another day."

"You let me worry about the shop."

"But you're spending all your time worrying about me."

"You'll last longer than the shop."

I did not like that she was resigned to closing down, but two days without any sales at all was going to severely damage her. I had a sudden thought. "What am going to tell Dad? I can't tell him I'm going to London with you."

"You can't just lie to him?"

"Lie? I've never lied to Dad."

"Every girl lies to their father."

"Not me." I instantly regretted saying that, for Jasmine had hidden the truth from her own father and he had died because of it. I wanted to apologise, but knew it would only make things worse.

Jasmine did not, however, seem to mind at all. "I'll talk with him," she said. "I'll tell him I need you to come visit a supplier with me."

"Then you'll be the one lying to him."

"Does that matter to you?"

I shifted where I lay. "I know this sounds stupid, but I don't like him being in the dark about stuff. This is the first time I've ever hidden anything from him. It's bad enough he doesn't know about the photos, but I don't want to get into a habit of bending the truth with him."

"Hold on, you've never hidden anything from him? Anything?"

"No. First girl I kissed, I told him that night."

"First girl you slept with?"

"Yep."

"Really?"

I nodded.

"OK, I can see how this is going to be a problem for you. We could take him with us."

I looked at her strangely, wondering whether she was serious. "I'll tell him I'm going to London with you," I said. "If he asks why, I'll say you're helping me with my problem."

"Will that be enough?"

"I think so, yeah."

"You have a great dad, Ro."

"Don't start with all that again."

We stayed on the beach for a while longer, soaking up the sun in silence, until I realised something was nagging at my mind.

"How did you know about the credit?" I asked. "The photographer credit on the magazine?"

"I bought the latest copy."

"You did? Why didn't I think of doing that?"

"It's pretty sordid, but each to their own."

I had another question to ask, but did not want to. Yet I knew I had no choice. "Was there ... Was I ...?"

"No. There were no pictures of you in there. None from Cara at all, although I was gambling they would use Cara's real name on the credits."

I heaved a sigh of relief. "Can I see the magazine?"

"Well, I don't have it on me. And this is a beach, it's for families."

"Yeah, didn't think. We should open the shop for a while, Jas."

"I suppose we should."

So that was what we did. For what was left of the afternoon, we returned to our ordinary life. We sold a few more of the sale items, did oddly well with beach-balls and even shifted three of the new kites which had been delivered. We stayed open later than we ordinarily would have and were somewhat surprised by how our fortune for the afternoon had changed.

As the evening air set in, we strolled back along the promenade, headed for Jasmine's house. It was strange, walking with her, for even with the wind blowing gently around us, everything was calm.

"You should phone your father," Jasmine said while we walked.

"I know. I just don't know what to tell him. It's been a while since I went to a girl's house to look through her porn mags."

Jasmine smiled. "That the sort of thing you usually get up to, Ro?"

"Back when I was a teenager, yeah."

"Did you tell your father about that as well?"

"You kidding?"

"I thought you didn't hide anything from him?"

"When I was a teenager, yeah, I hid all sorts of things. I meant I never hid anything from him once I hit sixteen."

"Sixteen's still a teenager, Ro."

"I never knew you were so pedantic, Jas."

"I can be a lot of things. I'm not just your cranky boss."

"You're not cranky. You just stress about work too much sometimes. Not saying you shouldn't, because money worries are awful, but it's not the be-all and end-all of life."

"Let's try to sort yours out first, eh?"

"I'm serious, Jas. I don't want to offend you, but you can't just lose yourself in work."

She glanced at me with an expression which was part sympathy, part mind-your-own-business. But there was nothing hurtful to her eyes at all. "Your father?" she said.

"Oh, right." I got out my phone and called him.

"Ro, how are you?"

"Good, Dad."

"I know I'm a good dad, but how are you?"

That made me laugh. It was the most comfortable I had been with him for a while. "I'll be home later, but I'm headed back to Jasmine's place for a while. There's something she wants to show me."

"Shall I keep dinner warm?"

My stomach rumbled at the suggestion of food. "Oh, yes please."

"Have you eaten today?"

"Jas and I had fish and chips on the beach."

"Any vegetables in there?"

"Not unless you count batter."

"Batter's not even remotely a vegetable."

"No, then."

"Is Jasmine still helping you?"

"Yes. Dad, I … I want to apologise for all the hurt I've caused you these last few days."

"Just go back to being the happy little ray of sunshine you've always been and we'll call it quits."

"I promise."

"I love you, Ro."

"Love you too, Dad."

I put away my phone and noticed Jasmine was staring out to the sea while we walked.

"We have that in common, you know," I said.

"What's that?"

"Looking out at the sea when we're sad."

"I was just thinking about my father. You have a lovely relationship with yours."

"Sorry."

"Don't be sorry, Ro." She stopped walking in order to face me. Taking my hands in hers, she gripped them tightly and I could see she was struggling with old memories – wounds which continued to fester even after so much time. "Just cherish what you have. Make the most of every moment, do whatever makes you happiest and promise me you'll never hide anything from the people you love."

She was hurting. It seemed she had been hurting for years. "I promise, Jas. You want to come round for dinner tonight? Dad's making pie."

"Are you still trying to set me up on a date?"

"I'm still torn between finding it icky and finding it wonderful."

"You don't think I'm too young for your father?"

"I don't think age matters much with love. It didn't work out with me and Cara because she's evil, not because she was a few years older than me."

"Your dad's more than a few years older than me, but thanks for thinking of me." She released my hands and we continued to walk. We did not speak, but we did not need to. The night was warm and in the morning we would put everything to bed. Jasmine was my saviour. Without her, I would already have thrown myself back into the sea.

# CHAPTER FOURTEEN

I spent a happy evening with my father. My sister was spending the night with one of her friends, for they had gone out to town as a group and had arranged to all stay at the same house. That was code to mean she was getting laid, but my sister was never one for telling Dad the truth. He never mentioned it, not to me anyway, and I often wondered why he never pulled her up on it.

We did not speak of much, which was nice. He did not pry, did not prod, and we laughed and joked and he insisted I eat three bowls of plum crumble, which was hardly a chore for me since I loved plum crumble.

Once we had eaten, he enveloped me in a massive hug and said, "I'm glad you have Jasmine to help you, Ro, but if you need anything from me, you just ask."

I hugged him back. He was my warm, steady rock and he would always be my hero. "I'll be fine," I said. "London's going to be fun."

"London?" he asked as we parted.

"Jas didn't mention it?"

"Why would Jasmine have to tell me?"

"She said she was going to call you." I thought back to our talk on the beach. A lot had happened since then; we had worked all afternoon, had a strange moment on the way back to her house and when we had got there, she had shown me the magazine she had bought. It was strange turning each page and fearing to see myself, but at least I was familiar with the magazine now. "I guess in all the excitement, she must have forgot," I said.

"What excitement?"

"I didn't mean excitement," I said quickly, thinking of the images in the magazine. "I meant work."

He looked at me strangely. "Is there something you want to tell me, Ro?"

"No," I said in a high-pitched voice.

"You're seeing an awful lot of Jasmine lately."

"I work with her."

"You keep going to her house. What did she want to show you today?"

"Oh, just a magazine."

"Which magazine?"

"A ... uh ..." I thought furiously for something to say and came up with nothing.

"And if I called Jasmine, she'd say she asked you back to her place to look at this magazine together?"

"Yeah."

"Would she be able to tell me which magazine it was?"

"Yeah. But please don't ask her, Dad. I don't lie to you, you know that. But please don't ask her."

He did not speak for several moments, then said, "I won't ask her. But no more secrets."

"Sure. Dad, what do you think of Jasmine?"

"She's swell. Why?"

"Oh, no reason. She's young and single, you know."

"Rowena, that is the worst attempt at matchmaking I've ever heard."

I winced. "Busted. Is there any more crumble?"

"For you, there's always more crumble. You'll turn *into* a crumble one day."

I ate more crumble and I could tell Dad was happy. My eating habits had been a bit off over the past few days and since he prided himself on his cooking, he was always pleased to see me eat well.

"What's in London, then?" he asked once I was done. "Or is that something I'm not allowed to know, either?"

"Pigeons."

"You're not going to London to see the pigeons."

"I'd better wash up."

"I'll wash up once you've gone. You tell me about London, then you'd best get to bed."

"What's in London?" I asked with a wince. "Londoners?"

He did not reply to that.

"Cara caused me some trouble," I said.

"I figured that much. Is she in London?"

"No. Jas and I went to see her today. I needed to square things with her."

"You didn't get into a fight, did you?"

"It wasn't that kind of visit. But London's the end for this, Dad. Jas is going to drive me down to London and then I can put Cara behind me forever."

"Whatever she did, why don't you just call the police?"

"That's our reserve. We can sort it better than the police could."

"Then what she did was illegal?"

"What I'm doing isn't. I'm not breaking any laws here, Dad, and I'm not getting into fights with anyone."

"I suppose that was more than I expected to get out of you. Go on, get ready for bed. I'll tidy up here."

"You sure, Dad? I can …"

"You can get some sleep. Sounds like you have a big day tomorrow."

I slept well that night, better than I had in a long while. The next morning, I said goodbye to my father and walked over to Jasmine's house. She wasn't quite ready so I waited on her settee while she got a bag together. I had brought my own sports bag, although Jasmine did not ask me what I had packed.

"I have snacks," she called from the kitchen. "And plenty of chocolate."

"Looking forward to our holiday already."

"Holiday?"

"Well, it's sort of like a holiday."

On the table before me were some papers and a notepad where Jasmine had scribbled a lot of figures. I glanced at them and saw they were the finances for the shop. Things were a lot worse than I feared.

"Ah, I was hoping you wouldn't see them," she said, coming into the room with her bag.

"I didn't mean to snoop."

"You're not snooping, Ro."

"How long do we have?"

"Not something we need to focus on right now. The shop's a lost cause, Ro, but you're not."

"Nor are you."

"Not starting up that debate again. Come on, car's waiting."

The drive to London took forever. My father had made me eat a large breakfast but I was hungry almost before we'd left Glazton. Jasmine said she had been working out her finances all morning and had only eaten a banana, so we stopped early on at a motorway café for lunch. I insisted on paying, which was difficult since Jasmine also insisted, but I won the argument and made sure Jasmine ate a sorbet for dessert. She liked sorbet almost as much as I loved my dad's plum crumble. Back in the car, we ate chocolate and chatted about nothing. Neither of us was hungry by that point, but we ate more through nerves than anything. If we kept that up, I would not fit into my bikini for much longer.

Eventually, we drove into London. It was like nothing I had expected.

London was huge and filled with so many narrow, winding roads it was as though it had not changed at all since Roman times. Great bridges spanned the River Thames, with pedestrians walking beside the traffic, none of them stopping to take in the sights. Cars crammed the roads, with more double-decker red buses than I had imagined could have existed outside of a television show. There were even some of the old-style London buses where everyone jumped onto the back where there was no door. There were chunky black taxis, too, although not as many as there were buses, with colourful adverts on their sides detracting somewhat from the iconic image.

The streets were varied, as well. Some were flat, others cobbled, and some seemingly designed with neither traffic nor pedestrians in mind. Nor was there any seeming sense to London, for there were side-streets visible everywhere, filled with quirky shops no one would ever see unless they already knew they were there.

The people were what shocked me the most. I did not know how many people there were in London, but it would not be an exaggeration to say I saw upwards of a million. Well, maybe a slight exaggeration, but it was still awesome.

There was no smog, but Cara was right in that the buildings did have a grey tint to them. I saw pigeons, but they did not stand in the road so I did not see much of them. From what I could tell, they certainly were not making to steal anyone's food.

I was reminded I had friends who lived in London, but we were not there to look them up. Besides, even if I called them and they told me where they lived, I imagined it would take another hour or more just to drive to them.

"I don't miss any of this," Jasmine said.

"You're from London?"

"Not Central London, but near enough. I used to come here to shop when I was a teenager. Well, Oxford Street anyway. My amateur dramatics studio's not too far from here."

I did not want to apologise again for bringing up her past. "I didn't know you'd run away to the seaside. I never really thought about it, but I guess I assumed you'd always lived there."

"I needed a new start. I needed to be somewhere no one knew me. London had too many familiar sights, too many sounds which brought back memories. I went to Glazton to make new memories."

"Like me with an ice cream on my head."

She laughed as she turned a corner in search of a parking spot.

"Jas, why did I have an ice cream on my head?"

"You don't remember?"

"No."

"I stuck it there. You were going on about some girl you'd met, you kept telling me how wonderful she was. I forget her name. Anyway, you were trying to hook me up with her older brother."

"Ha! I don't remember that at all, but it so sounds like me."

"You don't remember?" She sounded hurt.

"Sorry. Vaguely, I suppose. You didn't like her brother, I take it?"

"His name was Carlos, I remember that much."

"Carlos? Oh, Carlos, yeah. His sister was … ah, I forget her name. I was a little obsessed with her for a while, wasn't I?"

"For about three days, yeah. You remember Carlos but not his sister?"

"Carlos was a professional rugby player. I'd never seen anyone so well-built. He was gorgeous, you so should have gone out with him."

"Wasn't my type. There's one."

"One what?"

"A parking space."

Jasmine pulled the car in and fed the meter. I pulled out my sports bag to take with me and Jasmine eyed me curiously.

"You need all that stuff?" she asked.

"I have a secret weapon in here."

"Something you haven't shared with me?"

"Trust me, I could do without you trying to talk me out of it."

"OK. Just remember, Ro, this is going to be tough on you. These guys aren't going to scare as easily as Mr Tyler and his postcard factory."

"I won't be intimidated. I'm strong, Jas."

"I know you are. And you have me here all the way. You want me to take the lead?"

"No. Thank you, but no. I should talk to this Ms Yaren myself. If I can appeal to her better nature, I could get her to back down without this turning nasty."

"Ro, there's absolutely no way this isn't going to turn nasty."

"I know, but I'm still being optimistic. And if all else fails," I said, indicating my sports bag, "I have my backup plan."

"I'm still highly dubious about your backup plan, but I trust you. Still, no offense, but I'm taking the lead. No argument."

I offered no argument. It felt good having someone fight my corner for me like Jasmine was.

Walking the streets of London was not like being in the town where we had confronted Mr Tyler. I had thought that a big place, but London was like a whole different country. It was not simply that there were so many more people crammed into every square metre, nor was it that there were more people in the one street than I had ever seen in the whole of Glazton. There was a difference in attitude to London. There was certainly more aggression, but there was also a lack of recognition. No one spoke to each other, no one even looked at each other if they could help it. Everyone had their own lives to be getting on with and did not want to associate with all these others going about around them. I did not sense it was through fear, but simply because everyone was so focused on their own problems they did not care to include anyone else's.

I had heard that London was a stressful city and could certainly see why.

On the flipside, there were positive aspects to London. It was a diverse city which attracted not only tourists from around the world but also people who wanted to live there. Glazton was predominantly a white area, or at least it had been when I was a small child. Jasmine was evidence that there was some diversity, as was my own sexuality, but in London it did not seem to matter to anyone how people appeared or acted. Everyone was accepted mainly because everyone was ignored.

It would not be true, of course. No doubt the local news would be filled with bigotry and crime, but walking down those long, crowded streets, it was as though the whole city was one entity.

"This is the place," Jasmine said. We had arrived at a building where a sign outside read 'Greyliant Publishing' so this time the company owned the whole place. From the outside, there was nothing to suggest it was where dirty magazines were produced, and tens of thousands of people must have walked past it every day without knowing what went on inside.

There was a receptionist at the desk when we entered and we went through the routine of being asked our names all over again. When she heard who we were, she said we were expected and that we should go to the first floor. Nor was there a lift – it seemed some buildings in London were so old they had been constructed long before anyone cared about disabilities. The stairs were old and cold and we were grateful we only had to go one floor.

The office we entered was far more professional than I had expected. There were desks separated by small partitions over which staff could chat without having to stretch. There were offices with glass walls at the end of the room and it was to one of these I suspected we would be led. We were met by a woman younger than me and she asked us to follow her.

"There are a lot of women working here," I said as we did so.

"I've not noticed," she said. "I'm just a temp, I haven't been here long."

It was strange to think of it being like any other workplace, for I had imagined it would be a barely heated office, with lots of middle-aged men leering over the pages as they smoked cigarettes and laughed about the images. There were no nude pictures on the walls, not even in the cubicles, and I would have said around half the staff members were female.

No one paid us any attention as the temp led us to a glass office. There was a woman waiting within.

She was Japanese, short, with a craggy face filled with suspicion.

Jasmine extended her hand cordially and said, "Jasmine Chakma. Rowena Shelby. Ms Yaren?"

Yaren took the hand and motioned us to seats. I was nervous, my hands were sweating, but I set down my bag and sat with my legs together, my hands in my lap.

"Let's get this over with," Yaren said. "You've made some serious accusations about my publication and you're going to provide me with some proof."

"The proof's sitting next to me," Jasmine said. "All you have to do is compare her to the pictures you have."

Yaren pulled a flat cardboard file from a plastic rack on her desk. Opening it, she spilled out some of the photos Cara had taken of me. A few were of me wearing the blue swimsuit, but Yaren laid them out carefully, in sequence, to reveal the depraved show I had put on for Cara as I slowly stripped it off.

I shifted uncomfortably, for this was the first time Jasmine had seen them. Jasmine picked one up as though examining it and I wished she would just put it down – after all, she knew it was me in the photos. My bladder almost gave out when I saw there was one she had not noticed yet, one where I was pinching my nipple and forming my mouth into an O. I had tried to forget I had done those ones, but Cara had been very persuasive.

"These are the ones, yes," Jasmine said at last.

"So," Yaren said, "proof."

"They're obviously her."

"They're not obviously her. Maybe Ms Shelby has a twin sister. Do you have a sister?"

"Yes," I said without thinking, my eyes on the photos. "But she doesn't look anything like me. She's blonde."

"She could dye her hair. My problem, Ms Chakma, is that I have no evidence that these photos were sold to me without the consent of the model. I think it's pretty obvious there was no secret filming involved. The strip is a classic series of shots for magazines of our nature. They begin with the model fully clothed and end with her fully naked. All these photos tease the reader into watching her undress."

"Then why are there no fully naked ones?" Jasmine asked.

Here Yaren did at last look uncomfortable. "My freelancer didn't have any."

"Is that usual?"

"No."

"I wouldn't do it," I said. I had not known whether I would have been able to say anything else, but even though I felt as though I was about to die, I knew Jasmine was there to support me. Without her, I would never have had the courage to come to London at all. "I wouldn't do nude shots," I said. "Cara tricked me into even doing those. She said they were private, she said a lot of things. I thought she cared about me, I thought we had something."

"She tricked you with your emotions?" Yaren asked, pondering. "That's sneaky."

"I wasn't even comfortable wearing the swimsuit," I said. "It was tight, I could barely breathe. And she kept on at me, kept saying I didn't care about her, that

I had promised her and that I was ruining her chance and costing her money." I realised I was dribbling words and stopped.

"Strangely," Yaren said, "you still did it. And here we are."

"You've called her," Jasmine said calmly. "You must have called her. What did she say?"

"Not a lot. She said any financial matters between her and her models was none of my business. She's also right. Her story is that the girl who modelled for her signed the usual contract but then demanded more money after Ms Hughes and I made a deal for them. That's not done. If the model wants a bigger cut, she needs to air her concerns before the photos are sold, before she signs her own contract."

"I didn't sign anything," I said.

"Not my problem. Everything I did was legal. I bought photographs from a freelancer I've used before and have been assured the contract between photographer and model is valid. She's forwarded me the contract."

She produced another document and Jasmine took it. I did not read it but looked straight to the bottom, where my signature was displayed.

"Is that your signature?" Yaren asked.

"Yes," I said in a small voice.

"Then you signed the contract. It's not a copy: I had a courier fetch the original from Ms Hughes." Her eyes smiled. "I'm always very thorough."

"I didn't sign it," I cried. "She forged my signature. I signed her bear."

"Is that a euphemism?" Yaren asked.

"That's uncalled for," Jasmine snapped. I could see in her face that we were losing, that we had likely already lost. Cara had every angle covered. There was no way out for us.

"This isn't right," I said. "We'll call the police."

"Call them," Yaren said. "I'll show them the contract, you can confirm you're Rowena Shelby, which coincidentally is the same name as this signature, and they'll tell you off for wasting their time."

I bolted to my feet but Jasmine placed a hand on my arm. "You've had experience with this," she said icily to Yaren.

"Yes," she admitted. "Off the record, I'll tell you for free that I'm going to investigate this. I'm not using any more of Ms Hughes's work until I've conducted a thorough investigation. Tell anyone I said that and I'll deny it." Her face softened slightly. "I do feel for you, Ms Shelby, but at the end of the day I run a business and my priority is protecting it. This company employs a lot of people and accusations like this could ruin us."

"What about me?" I asked coldly. "What about ruining me?"

"If you don't want nude photos of yourself leaked to the world, I suggest you don't pose for them."

With tears in my eyes, I grabbed my sports bag and fled. Jasmine called after me, but I did not stop. Barrelling through the office, I caused heads to turn. Some people laughed, others whispered, a few may even have known who I was but I doubted it. Behind, I could hear Jasmine calling, the pain evident in her voice, but I could not stop.

Hurling myself through the door to the ladies', I locked myself into a cubicle and clenched my eyes to blot out the tears. The last time I had locked myself in a toilet cubicle, I had wept fiercely without hope. Now I had Jasmine, but I also had a secret weapon. The time for crying was over. Opening my sports bag, I took a deep breath and decided I would have to embrace my sin.

# CHAPTER FIFTEEN

Jasmine was shouting when I returned to the office. Ms Yaren was standing calmly, taking all the abuse because she knew there was nothing either of us could do against her. She had the law on her side, and the more Jasmine shouted, the more control Yaren had over the situation. All the staff were watching, some were not bothering to hide the fact, and I was able to walk a few paces into the office before anyone noticed me. When they did, no one was interested in watching the angry shouting woman any more, for there was suddenly something more engaging to focus on.

There were a few smiles, but mainly the room was filled with confusion. My knees threatened to give out at any moment, but I had used the toilet while in the cubicle so there was little chance of me losing control of my bladder. I was not calm, I was about as far from calm as I could have been, but I gained strength from knowing I would not have to face this alone.

When Jasmine saw me, she stopped shouting. Her mouth remained open as though she didn't know whether to continue, but her eyes widened in shock. I offered her a smile and a little wave. Dumbly, she waved back.

I was barefoot, for my shoes and clothes were all stashed in the sports bag I had left by the door. My smooth tanned legs were naked, as were my arms. The tight-fitting blue swimsuit which had been at the centre of all my problems hugged my skin, clutching me like a lost lover recently rediscovered. On my head I wore the white captain's cap with its black visor and golden tassels. Movement was difficult in the thing, but the more steps I took, the more my confidence grew. I was fully aware that the tight material pinched my bum cheeks and exposed their lower halves, just as I was aware the waterproof blue material pressed against me to enhance the curves of my breasts and the smoothness of my belly. My red curls bounced gaily, happy to be back in such a state, just as they had been during the actual shoot.

"Ro," Jasmine finally whispered. "Ro, what are you doing?"

"I completely agree," Yaren said. "Your signature has already established that you're the same woman in the photos, you don't need to parade yourself like this."

"I'm not parading," I said. "I'm showing you where your photos come from."

"I know where they come from, thanks."

"And, signature or no signature, if I go running out into the street like this, crying, what do you think will happen?"

Yaren's eyes narrowed.

"If I was, say," I continued airily, "to scream about how I was being used, how I was being forced to wear this tight costume, how I had been forced to scribble my signature on a piece of paper. How do you think that might go down with the police? Do you still think they'd tell me off for wasting their time?"

Yaren was about ready to explode. Her face was so red she reminded me of a lobster on the boil.

"It's a shame you sent a courier to fetch the original contract," I said. "It means I could say I was forced to sign it here, in this building. If Cara had just e-mailed you a copy, you'd have a chance to win this. But then, you're always very thorough."

I stared at her, waiting for her to make the next move. Jasmine said nothing, for she knew full well there was nothing she could say, either.

A moment later, Yaren's face broke out into a grin. "Oh, this is too much. I applaud your bravado, Ms Shelby. It's not often I'm outmatched. I'm used to crossing swords with lawyers. Looking at you now, I can hardly believe you were talked into anything you didn't want to do."

"I'm not the same person I was a couple of weeks ago," I said.

Yaren placed her hands on her hips and did not hide her grin. "All right, you've won. I'll pull the pictures. We'll use something else."

"Pull them?" I asked. "You mean recall the magazines?"

"Recall them? We haven't printed them yet."

My heart skipped a beat at those words. "You haven't printed them?"

"Printing magazines doesn't happen overnight, Ms Shelby. The photo-strip of you is ready to go, but nothing's hit the printers yet. We're still a couple of months away from featuring you. It's a shame, because we were going to use you on the cover. Hughes got a good bonus for that, let me tell you."

"Not printed," I said, hardly believing what I was hearing. My father would never have to see the topless photos of me. I had taken Cara's copies and the only other person who had any of them was Ms Yaren. I was safe, my shame was hidden. My father was spared.

I looked to Jasmine and saw the happiness bursting from her face. Rushing across the office, I threw my arms about her and she embraced me tightly. A couple of people in the office clapped and one woman sighed heavily.

"If you're done," Yaren said, "let's step back into my office so I can deal with those photos for you."

We followed in a daze and once in her office, I sank into a chair. The swimsuit did not like me sitting anywhere and it pulled even tighter against me, but I did not care. I watched as Yaren typed on her computer and called up all the photos she had of me.

"Now," she said, "I can delete them, but there goes the evidence. Without the photos, I'm going to have a hard time chasing Hughes for a refund."

"She doesn't have any money, anyway," I said. "She doesn't even have any furniture."

"One for the lawyers to sort out, then," she said as she hit the key to delete them.

"Out of interest," Jasmine said cautiously, "why did you do that? If it's going to cost you money, why didn't you keep the pictures and take Cara to court?"

Yaren gathered up her paper copies and placed them on the table in one bundle. "Firstly, it's only money. Magazines like mine have a bad reputation and taking hits like this isn't good for business. If I lose a little money to a freelancer without morals but don't get the bad press, I'm good with that. Secondly, like I said, that's for lawyers to sort out. Greyliant has some of the best lawyers, we have to, and here at Wet Daydreams we don't cause them half the headaches some of the other departments do. They owe us a little leeway. Thirdly, most importantly, I'm not often put in my place. When I am, I know to back down."

"Thank you," I said and found I meant it. "I was all ready to hate you, Ms Yaren. To plead with you, to threaten you, to … I don't know what else I was going to do. But you're not bad."

She grunted. "Don't let that get around the office, Shelby." She leaned back in her chair. "You know, not that I'm saying I agree with her methods, but I can see why Hughes deceived you. You fill out that swimsuit like a pro, Shelby. Fancy some legitimate work?"

"You mean take my clothes off and get paid for it? No thanks."

"If you ever change your mind, give me a call. You'd make me a fortune."

I knew she was exaggerating, but I did not mind at all. My nightmare was over and I could breathe again. Or at least, I would be able to just as soon as I got changed.

"We've done it," I said to Jasmine. "The nude photos were never published and the postcards have been pulled. I'm clear."

"Postcards?" Yaren asked. "What postcards? We don't print postcards."

"The Captain's Bombshell," Jasmine said.

"The who what?"

Jasmine produced something from her pocket. I had not realised she had been carrying it around with her and wasn't sure how I felt about it. She passed the postcard over to Yaren, who took it and examined it with narrowed eyes.

"This is the same costume," she said.

"I only did it the once," I squealed. "Well, twice now," I added, aware I was wearing the costume presently.

Yaren set down the card and sorted through her own photos. She found one of precisely the same image as that on the card. "We were going to use this," she said. "The photo's amazing. The coyness, the lightly brushing of fingers on the thigh." She shook away her daydreams – it seemed I was not the only one who suffered from that. "Hughes sold me these pictures. The same pictures she sold to this other company."

"Those pictures are on the Internet already," I said.

"Are they now?" she asked with narrowed eyes. Turning to her computer, she ran a search and scowled. "Ms Shelby, with your permission I'd like to keep a few of these hard copies. I want to show them to our lawyers. They're proof that Hughes sold exactly the same photo to two different companies. The similar ones we have add extra weight to the charge."

"She'd get in serious trouble for that, wouldn't she?" I asked.

"Ro," Jasmine cautioned. "Ro, please stop being so lenient to her. Cara almost got you killed."

"I know. But that's because she's a monster. If I did this, she might go down that same route." Taking the photos, I drew them towards me. "I'm sorry, Ms Yaren, but Cara has nothing. No one loves her, no one likes her, no one even has a kind word to say about her. All she has is debt and that's no one's friend. I can't do this to her."

"I can't slap her with a big lawsuit without those photos," Yaren cautioned. "If she has so much debt already, taking those photos away from me will only prolong her suffering. Plus, she'll be living in constant fear that one day I'll come for her."

I shrugged as I stood, photos in hand. "Then she should have thought of that before she screwed with my emotions."

Yaren cackled with glee. "I'm liking you more all the time, Shelby."

"She has that effect on people," Jasmine said as she too rose.

As we walked back through the office, a couple of people applauded. I performed a slight bow to them, much to Jasmine's consternation, but the fact of the matter was I was ludicrously happy. Collecting my sports bag, I returned to the toilet cubicle to change back into my proper attire before Jasmine and I left the building and returned to the street.

We breathed in deeply of the thick London air. It was filled with car fumes and tarmac, of people and stress. It was not like Glazton at all.

"It's over," I said. "All thanks to you."

"I think you deserve some credit there, Ro."

"Let's go shopping."

"Shopping?"

"We're in London, Jas, we have to go shopping. I'm going to buy you an ornamental pig."

"Ro, you don't have to buy me a pig."

"I know." Crooking my arm, I offered it to her. "Shall we?"

For the rest of the afternoon, we went shopping. London was big, loud and sometimes scary. We visited Trafalgar Square and sat on the paws of a lion while we tried to count the pigeons; we were awed by how Covent Garden could fit in not only stalls but also narrow doorways with shops above; we visited the many London tourist shops and picked up a few tips on how to sell local tat; we tried to find Harrods and instead ended up in Hamleys, which was probably no cheaper but much more fun.

We must have spent an hour just in Oxford Street alone, and somewhere along the way we had lunch, which Jasmine insisted on buying. When we eventually became exhausted, we decided to call it a day. We had bought very little, mainly because neither of us had much money, although I had managed to find the pig ornament I had promised Jasmine. It was a solar-powered bobbing thing which moved its head from side to side when the sun shone on it. Personally, I thought the thing would be annoying, but Jasmine said she loved it.

On the way back to the car, I noticed Jasmine had stopped and I looked back to see what she was looking at. We had not been through the West End, yet there were theatres everywhere in London. The one at which Jasmine had stopped was like any other. From the outside, it was an old building and inside it was likely grand. There was a comedy being shown, but I had never heard of it; nor did I recognise any of the actors. But it was neither the content nor the actors which had drawn Jasmine's attention, for I could see such sadness in her eyes as she looked at the entrance.

"Jas," I said, not quite sure what to say. "You can't dwell on the past."

"I know. It's just, we've solved your problem, Ro. The only copies of the nude photos are now on a USB drive in your pocket. Cara's out of your life forever, and if Mr Tyler manages to recall all those postcards, you don't even have to worry about those. We've won, Ro. Your life can go back to normal, and I'm happy for you, I really am. It just makes me think of what I lost, of what I could have had. I was fifteen when I lost my dream, Ro. That was over half my lifetime ago. If I was strong, like you, I could have fought my shame. I could have admitted to my father what had happened. He probably would have blamed me, but he sure as hell would have gone after that director with a cricket bat."

"How can you say you're not strong, Jas? If not for you, I'd be dead. Literally. I'd have jumped straight back into the sea until the lifeguards got fed up of pulling me out. Or I would have found some other way to kill myself. You saved my life, Jas, and you say you're not strong?"

She rubbed at her eyes with thumb and forefinger and my heart broke for her.

Taking her hands in mine, I forced her to look at me. I had never seen her in such pain and there was nothing I could do. "Jas, you lost your dream, but if you hadn't, you never would have come to Glazton. I never would have met you, and I never would have been able to do all of this by myself. These last three years working in your shop have been the happiest I've ever known. When my mother died, I remember crying a lot. I still miss her, but I don't remember all that much about her any more. It's sad to admit, but sometimes I can't even picture her face. I'd never admit that to Dad, but it doesn't stop it being true. When my friends all moved away, I was left with my one true love – the sea. It was the only thing which ever understood me.

"And then I met you. You gave me a job, a purpose. I was earning my own money, I could pay my way. But you gave me something else, Jas. You gave me someone to look up to, someone to care about. You've always been there for me. Whenever I hit the rocks, whenever I go through a nasty break-up, whenever I just need someone's shoulder to cry on, you're always there. You don't judge me, you don't hassle me, you don't question. You just listen and sometimes you offer me advice. Advice which is always perfect.

"I'm not saying it's a good thing what happened to you. I would never say that. But from something bad came something beautiful, Jas. Because if all that horror and pain hadn't happened to you, we never would have met; and my life would have been miserable."

All the while I was talking, she never once broke eye contact. And I had watched as slowly her sadness faded. It was not replaced with happiness, but there was certainly something else there. Longing, I would have called it, although I had no idea what she was longing for.

"Ro," she said, "you always did have such a fantastic way with words."

"I speak from the heart. My dad says I'm good at that because I have a big heart."

"You have a beautiful heart."

I felt a flush of warmth that she had said such a thing and squeezed her hands where I was still holding them. "Jas, just tell me what I can do to help and I'll do it. I don't care what it is, just tell me and it's done."

"There is something."

"Done."

"It's just not something I've ever wanted to say. I've known you a long time, Ro, and I'm ... afraid of you."

"Afraid of me?"

"You're so fun and gorgeous and sweet. And so young as well. I didn't feel right in saying anything before, but after all this business with Cara, I ... well, I'm only a year older than Cara, Ro."

I did not know what she was saying, but it was certainly true that she was only a year older than Cara. Then it hit me. "Oh, I understand."

"You do?" she asked with nervous relief.

"You mean because I was attracted to Cara, right? Even though she's older than me."

"That's precisely what I'm talking about, Ro," she said excitedly.

"And Cara was my dream, and the theatre's your dream. You're saying you think you're still young enough to get back on stage."

"I am?"

"Absolutely. Oh, Jas, I'm so happy for you. When we get home, we can look into it together. There must be amateur acting in Glazton. We have that little theatre, right? They have to do something you can be a part of. And, once they see you perform, they'll snap you up in an instant."

"Ro, that wasn't what I ..."

"I'm so happy for you." I emitted a shriek of sheer bliss which drew a few stares. Releasing Jasmine's hands, I skipped ahead, full of the promise of Jasmine's future. I had spent so long trying to think of a way to help her, to make her happy, that I had brushed over something as simple as helping her get started on a new acting career. It all made sense, it was so obvious I should have seen it sooner.

We returned to the car. Our holiday was over and we drove back to Glazton, stopping for dinner in a motorway café. I insisted on paying again, although I could not help but notice Jasmine was morose throughout. I decided she was just nervous at the thought of getting back on stage, yet I strangely knew that wasn't the problem at all.

Whatever was bothering her, though, we would sort it. Together, we could have taken on the world.

# CHAPTER SIXTEEN

We did not arrive back in Glazton until about six and I was surprised at how tired I was. Jasmine dropped me off at home and I thanked her all over again for everything she had done.

"Just glad to see you happy again," she said.

"You want to come in for a while?" I asked as I unbuckled my seat belt. "Dad might have made some more crumble."

"I'd love to, Ro, but I'm tired and I'd best get home."

"Back to an empty house and depressing finances to work through? That's not a fun evening, Jas. And I definitely owe you a fun evening."

"Trying to set me up with your father is not a fun evening, Ro."

"I was only ever really half serious about that, you know."

"Good. Because relationships with vast age differences never work."

"Like I said before, age doesn't matter much with love, Jas."

She looked like she wanted to say something, but instead was silent. She had been doing that a lot lately and I wondered whether I was making things worse for her.

Reaching over to the back seat, I grabbed my bag and said, "Not just ten minutes?"

"Best not. You have a lot to talk about with your father. I'm not family, I'd only get in the way."

"You're not family?" I asked. "You honestly think that?"

"I'm not going to get all mopey with you, Ro, but I don't have a family. We're friends, Ro, and that's all. I'm not your mother, I'm not your sister, and I'm not going to pretend to be any other part of your family."

She was staring straight ahead as she spoke, her hands gripping the wheel, and all over again I knew I had upset her somehow.

"Jas," I said, "including everything that's happened these past couple of weeks, that has to be the most soul-destroying thing anyone's ever said to me."

She glanced at me. "Things are how they are, Ro. Go on, your dad's waiting."

"Jas, I can't leave you like this."

"Like what? Alone?"

"You're sad. I don't like to see my best friend sad. We both know what happens when either of us gets miserable and it ends with someone pumping our chests."

I reached out to brush a loose strand of hair from her forehead and she pulled away. "It was a long time ago that I took all those pills," she said. "It's not a route I'm going down again. Don't worry about me."

"How can I not worry about you? I care about you, Jas."

She looked at me properly then. Her eyes were unwavering, even if they were uncertain. "You'll have to find a new job, Rowena. When the shop goes under, I'll have a lot of problems, but you might want to start looking now. Maybe you should start looking tomorrow."

"Tomorrow? I have work tomorrow. The more we sell, the more money we make for when things get really bad for you."

"I can handle the shop. You need to look after yourself now. I'm a lost cause. I need to let you go. The shop," she amended, her eyes glistening. "I meant the shop's a lost cause. And that *you* need to let *me* go."

"I'm not leaving you."

"It's going to be difficult enough as it is without you working with me."

"You mean because of paying me? I'll work for free. Technically, you fired me anyway, so I shouldn't be paid. I have to work off the cost of those glass statues at the very least."

"Ro, please."

"Jas, I'm not abandoning you when you need me the most."

"I don't need you," she said, angrily wiping away a tear. "The shop's gone, I don't care about it any more. I'm moving away."

"You what?"

"There's nothing for me here in Glazton now. Just memories."

"Good memories?"

"Good and bad. Thank you for being there, Ro. Thank you for listening to me when I told you about my father and my ... incident. But I shouldn't have burdened you with any of it. The truth is, I never liked Glazton to begin with. I'm a Londoner, and if today's taught me one thing, it's that I should go back there. I can start small, get back into amateur dramatics. Who knows, a couple of years from now I could be in one of those West End theatres."

"Jas, you can't mean that." Something cold stabbed my heart at the very thought of what she was saying. All my life I had daydreamed, but suddenly there were no images, no visions swimming around my mind. Without Jasmine, there simply was no dream. "Jas, I can't imagine you not being in my life."

"You won't have to imagine it for much longer, Ro. Please get out the car and go home. I'm very tired and I want to go to bed."

"Jas, I ..."

"Ro?"

I was speechless and opened the door. I stood there for some moments, still trying to think of something to say, trying to find words which would make everything all right again. But there was nothing. I closed the door and stepped back as Jasmine pulled away from the kerb and drove out of my life.

I stood there watching after her for a long time. Always would I be able to imagine something, but the dreams were still not coming. Every scenario which ordinarily would have popped into my head unbidden was buried deep under the great pressure pushing down on my heart. The future was gone and all I had left were memories. Lying on the beach eating fish and chips, eating breakfast with her and turning down her extra sausage, working in the shop and almost dropping her laptop, even sitting in her living-room looking through that dodgy magazine. Above all, there was one image burned into my mind: that of the two of us posing for the camera, me with an ice cream on my head.

Veronica. I remembered her name then. She was the sister of Carlos the rugby player. Jasmine had stuck an ice cream on my head because I had tried to hook her up with Carlos while I was pining over Veronica. How could I have forgotten Veronica? I also recalled why I had pined over her. She was a girl I had instantly fallen for, but she wasn't interested in me because all she could talk about was Jasmine. She had obsessed about Jasmine just as I had obsessed about Veronica, which had made it an uncomfortable time for all of us. I remembered I kept telling Veronica that Jasmine wasn't gay, that there was no point chasing after her. and Veronica kept rolling her eyes at me and said if I wasn't getting anywhere, I should be prepared to give someone else a chance.

That was the whole reason I had tried to set Jasmine up with Carlos in the first place, to prove to Veronica that Jasmine was straight. After all, no heterosexual girl would ever turn down the chance of spending time with Carlos.

My plan had backfired when Jasmine had wanted nothing to do with Carlos.

There was something there, something I wasn't seeing. I fought frantically for the answer, for I knew there was something plainly obvious staring me in the face, some reason Jasmine was so unhappy, yet I could not quite ...

A horn blared behind me and I realised I was standing in the road. Leaping out of the way, I allowed the car to pass. If this was London, the driver would likely have honked at me all over again, but in Glazton people tended not to do that.

With a solemn sadness, I opened my front door and went home. Walking into the living-room, I dropped my bag and sunk into the settee. The pictures were dealt with and I was safe, yet I had never been more miserable.

"Ro, you're home," Dad said as he entered with two steaming cups.

"Hot chocolate?" I asked. It was strange to think everyone knew how much I loved hot chocolate.

"There's some more plum crumble, too, if you want it," he said as he perched himself on the edge of a chair.

"Maybe tomorrow. I don't feel like eating right now."

"How was London?"

"Fine."

"Did you get everything sorted?"

"Yes. The problem's solved. Cara's out of my life forever and everything's good."

"Then why are you so sad?"

"Jasmine's leaving."

"Leaving?"

"The shop's finished. She's packing up and leaving. She's going back to London."

"She won't be able to afford to live in London if she doesn't have any money."

"Maybe she's running away from her debt, I don't know." I rubbed at my eye. "I can't think straight, Dad. I can't lose her."

"You'll find another job."

"Forget the job, it's Jas I'm worried about. She …" I realised I could not tell him anything about her past, for they were not my secrets to tell. "She's told me some things about herself. About her past. She's such a sad woman, Dad, and I don't know how to help her."

"Maybe you can't. Maybe no one can."

"You don't know what she went through."

"No. People come to Glazton to retire, they do it all the time. Or they come here to live a quiet life. Jasmine's not of a retirement age and she doesn't strike me as someone who wants to live a quiet life."

"She wants to be left alone, forgotten."

"But she has an entrepreneurial streak about her."

"I know. It conflicts with everything else that makes her who she is."

"I'm sure she'll sort out her own problems."

"Don't you see? She's spent so long helping me, she's suffering herself. Now I have to help her. I have to, Dad."

"Maybe you could do some modelling for her."

"Maybe not. My modelling days are …"

My voice trailed off. He looked at me in silence.

"You know, don't you?" I asked in a small voice.

In answer, he took something from the sideboard. It was a postcard I had hoped would have somehow disappeared into the ether. My father sat in silence, waiting me to explain.

"They don't make them any more," I said in a calmer voice than I had expected. "We spoke with the company and they've stopped production."

"So you did know about them, then."

I did not want to say the next word, but I had no choice. "Yes."

"Did Jasmine put you up to it?"

"Jas?"

"I was on the verge of phoning the police when I saw it. A friend of mine showed it me, I couldn't believe it. If you'd done something like that, you would have told me. But it was you in the picture, so I had to assume Jasmine put you up to it."

"Jasmine helped me, Dad."

"Are you sure? She's desperate, Ro. Maybe it's a good thing she's leaving, if she's leaving at all."

"I know she has money worries, Dad, but she would never do something like that to me."

"Then tell me."

That was precisely what I did. We sat for over an hour as I explained everything that had happened. I left nothing out. I started with when I had met Cara in the shop and sold her some green sandals she had hated. I told him about Sophie warning me and me not listening, of how I had waited all night for Cara and did not eat. I told him about the pier and the hook-a-duck and the bumper cars. He did not say a word when I went through the whole incident on the beach, where Cara and I had shared an intimate kiss for almost an hour while she cemented our relationship. I thought I would hold back when I revealed everything that had happened at the studio, but I didn't. Nor did he react as I described my light-headed sweatiness in that swimsuit, and of how my emotions and lack of oxygen had enabled Cara to take advantage of me.

After this, I was only vaguely aware my father was in the room with me and I went on to describe everything that had happened since. How I had destroyed Jasmine's most expensive stock, how she had fired me, how I had felt so down and desperate and alone that I had jumped into the sea and wished I was dead. How the lifeguards had rescued my body and how Jasmine had rescued my soul.

I told him of the trip to the postcard printers, to confront Cara, and finally our long journey to the London office of the pornographic magazine. And I told him of how Jasmine had brought me home, how she had all but refused to leave my side since my suicide attempt.

When I was done, when I found there were no further words to be said, I fell silent and cradled my cold cup of hot chocolate.

The room was silent.

My father carefully set down his own mug and sat beside me upon the settee. Gently, he placed his arms about me and still he said nothing. I was tense, uncertain, and my mug fell from shaking fingers, spilling cold chocolate all over the carpet. Clinging to my father, I wept as he did and there we remained for an eternity.

When we were done, my eyes stung and my throat was tight, but I somehow knew those had been the final tears to be shed over the whole sorry mess.

"I'm sorry for not telling you sooner, Dad," I said.

"Just never do anything like this again, all right?"

"I'm sworn off stupidity, I promise."

Sitting up, my father controlled his breathing and picked up the postcard again. "Funny thing is, it's not even a bad picture."

"How can you say that?"

"It's not. Yeah, it's not exactly what I'd expect from you, but if this was your sister in this picture, I would have just shrugged it off as something she probably gets up to anyway."

"Dad, don't talk like that."

"Rowena, look at it. Really look at it. Yes, we can see your legs and your arms, but those aren't things you've ever hidden before."

"I know, but my ... well, my ..."

"Your bum's showing to the camera, you can say it. It's also covered."

"Half covered."

"Half covered. You're covered where it counts. I've seen a lot worse in my time, even on postcards."

It was not how I had thought he was going to react and I said, "Are you saying I should be happy with it?"

"No. I'm saying if this was a legitimate direction you wanted your life to go in, yes you should be happy with it. But since Cara sold these images without your consent, of course you shouldn't be happy with it."

"If I ... you mean you'd have been happy for me if I'd chosen to do this?"

"Not really. Like I said, I'd expect this from your sister. But you're twenty-two, Ro. You're not a child and I should stop thinking of you as one. You're an adult and you're allowed to make your own decisions.

There's nothing illegal about these images and there's decent money to be made in modelling. It's just not you."

"I never thought about it like that before." Yet the more I did think about it, the more his words made sense. There was nothing vulgar about being a model, there was nothing disreputable about being photographed wearing a swimsuit. He was right in that it was not in my character to pose for such pictures, yet the simple truth of the matter was that I *had* posed for them. Willingly. Whether they were sold was irrelevant, because I had known full well the pictures were being created. Just as when I had sat in a photo booth with Cara, or when I had that ice cream on my head with Jasmine. I had known those photos were being taken, it was just that they were not being commercially distributed.

It meant I had done nothing wrong. Jasmine had been right all along. I was a victim and I had nothing to be ashamed of.

It also gave me an idea.

"I love you, Dad."

"You've been saying that a lot lately. It's come to mean you have another secret you're keeping from me."

"Oh, I have an idea, but it's not a secret." I told him of my idea. He listened intently. The more I explained it, the more he warmed to the notion, although I could tell he was not entirely comfortable with it.

"Like I said," he said, "you're an adult. Just remember, even though you're no longer my little girl, you'll always be my little girl."

"And you're the best dad ever."

"It looks like I have an apology to make to Jasmine, then."

"Why? What have you said to her?"

"Nothing. But I've blamed her for all of this. You've gone running to her a lot lately, been staying over her house and everything. I thought she was trying to take advantage of you, but it looks as though she's genuinely concerned."

"Of course she's concerned. She's my boss and my best friend. And what do you mean, taking advantage of me? You mean making me work long hours? That's just because I've been trying to save her business."

"No, I meant taking advantage of you as a woman."

I frowned. "I'm not following."

"You know, because she's a woman and you're a woman? I thought she was preying on you because you're naïve and gullible and sweet as the plum crumble I still have in the kitchen if you want any."

"Sweet as the ... Aw, I'm not that sweet. And I know we're both women, thanks, but what are you talking about?"

He blinked, taken aback. "You honestly have no idea what I'm saying, do you?"

"Well, if you'd stop talking in riddles, I might get an idea."

"I mean because she has a massive crush on you. I think she's probably in love with you, although she never seems to have said it."

I stared at him, aghast. Then I laughed. I laughed so loudly I almost cried again. "Oh, Dad, you're so clueless. Jasmine's not in love with me. She's not a lesbian."

"You sure?"

"Of course I'm sure." I thought about the one man with whom I knew she had been intimate, but he did not count because he had assaulted her. I stopped laughing, because I couldn't think of anyone else she had ever shown any interest in. "Carlos," I said then. "Carlos was a rugby player."

"Her boyfriend?"

"No, she didn't look twice at him, actually. She dumped an ice cream on my head when I wouldn't stop going on about his sister."

My father raised his eyebrows.

"No," I said, rolling my eyes. "She didn't do it because she was jealous. And she lives alone because of something bad that happened to her in the past. She's allowed to avoid relationships without being gay, Dad."

"Why is she leaving Glazton?"

"The shop's gone and all she has left are bad memories."

"She's not running away because you rejected her?"

I laughed again. "I didn't reject her."

"You sure?"

I thought back over the past few days, but had been concerned with my own problems and had paid little attention to how Jasmine had been acting around me. Then I remembered when we had been outside the theatre, when she had tried to confess something and I had assumed she was talking about being on stage. And I remembered the car, before I had come into the house. The car, where she had said she wouldn't ever be a part of my family, when she had been shaking and on the verge of tears as she said she had to let me go.

Her words from the beach returned to me just as easily as Cara's had right before I jumped from the pier.

"Cherish what you have," Jasmine had said. "Make the most of every moment, do whatever makes you happiest and promise me you'll never hide anything from the people you love."

My mouth fell agape as I realised the truth that had been slapping me in the face for months, the truth I had been daydreaming too much to ever see.

"Oh," I said. It's entirely possible I swore as well because my father looked a little shocked. "Sorry," I said. "Actually, I think sorry's become my favourite word lately. Why'd she never tell me? Why's she never say anything at all?"

"Clearly, sharing her emotions is difficult for her. Whatever this terrible thing in her past is, could it have something to do with why she's withdrawn when it comes to relationships?"

I nodded in silence.

"Then there's the age gap," he said. "She's nine years older than you. She probably thought it wasn't a good idea to tell you how she felt because you'd laugh at her, or run a mile or something. Plus, she's your boss."

"And when I fell for Cara," I said, the pieces falling into place, "she saw age didn't matter to me. And she still didn't say anything because she has about as much self-respect as a ... well, as a girl who strips naked for magazines."

"How do you feel about her?"

"I don't know." It was true. Everything was happening so quickly, I did not have time to sort through my emotions. "I love her, there's no doubt about that. But I don't know whether I'm *in* love with her. I mean, she's kind and gentle and listens to me when I have problems and ... Oh my God, I always cry on her shoulder when I break up with girls and she never says a word. She just listens, offers me a bed for the night and makes me feel better."

My father sighed as he stood. "You have a lot to think about. I'm going to get something to sponge out the chocolate in the carpet. Take your time, Ro. Think hard about things, there's no rush. You want some crumble?"

"No," I said, my emotions a mass of confusion. My stomach was churning, my heart was racing and my mind was reeling. "No, thanks."

He patted my knee. "Take all night, Ro, but talk to Jasmine in the morning. You owe her that much."

That night I lay in bed, staring at the ceiling. My problems with the photos may have been over, but Jasmine's problems were what was important. In the grand scheme of things, all I had were raunchy pictures and nude ones which had now been supressed. Jasmine had a love she was terrified to confess.

It broke my heart to think of her in pain, and as I lay awake all night thinking about her, I knew the solution was to stop thinking. For thinking was something you did with your brain, while love came only from the heart.

And my heart had already made the decision for me.

# CHAPTER SEVENTEEN

I had not slept, so should not have had any energy the following morning, but I was so fired up I doubted I would sleep for a week. Rising early, I went straight down to the shop to get things prepared. On the way, I made a call and arranged something. Only an hour later, my special delivery arrived, by which time I had organised the shop to sell the maximum amount of stock. I removed all the sale stickers, for I had a feeling today was going to be a good day for trade.

By the time Jasmine arrived, looking sullen and defeated, I had a bustling, thriving business going. I watched her approach, my heart fluttering in anticipation of how she would react, at what she might say or do. She was staring at the floor, hands in her pockets, while she walked, and only looked up when she noticed the commotion. She frowned at the score of people in the shop, for it had been some time since we had even six in there at once.

Then she saw me, behind the counter, and she stopped walking. Her eyes widened and her jaw dropped. For one horrible moment I thought she was going to turn on her heel and walk briskly away, for I could see the possibility flit across her eyes. Instead, she steeled her resolve and came towards me.

"Rowena?" she asked. "What are you doing?"

"Morning, Jas," I said with a broad grin.

I was wearing the blue swimsuit I had taken from Cara. It was as tight as ever, but that was part of the appeal. Atop my head I wore the white captain's cap, my red curls bouncing gaily upon my shoulders. On the wall behind me was plastered my special delivery: a massive poster depicting the image Cara had taken, the swimsuit photograph which had been sold to Charm Pictures. Across the counter I had stacks of postcards, while there were even more on the revolving racks I had put back in.

"Ro," Jasmine said, more forcefully, "what are you doing?"

"I spoke with my dad last night. Told him everything. He knew some of it, one of his friends gave him a postcard. And you know what? He said there was nothing wrong with it. The image, I mean. What Cara did was wrong, but he wasn't ashamed of me. I was ashamed of myself, but he didn't hate me for it."

"Ro, the poster? The swimsuit?"

She stepped back as someone bought a few sticks of rock, a small model boat and a postcard. He asked me to sign it and I did so with a wink.

"Ro," Jasmine said when he was gone, "this isn't you."

"No, Jas, this *is* me. I sit on the beach in my bikini, I find quiet places to lie naked so I can get a proper tan, and I get squeamish when people see a photo of me in a swimsuit? This is a moneymaker, and if my dad doesn't feel ashamed of me, then there's nothing for me to feel ashamed about."

"All right, don't be ashamed. Just stop winking at the customers. It's creepy."

"I'm not winking at … Did I wink at that guy? Oops."

Jasmine held her head with both hands. "I can't deal with this, Ro. The shop's going under, I can't have you parading yourself like this just to help me out."

Another customer bought a postcard and this time I signed it without winking at him.

"I'm not going to let anyone tell me what I can and can't do, Jas. I keep telling everyone I'm twenty-two, but no one seems to listen. I'm my own woman and can make my own decisions. And I'm not just helping you out. I work here, so I have a stake in how well we do. Besides, the shop's not going under."

"Ro, I owe the bank a lot of money. You'd have to sell a shedload of postcards to make any sort of dent in that."

"How many?"

"A lot."

"Good, because we've sold a lot. We've been open for three hours now, you took your time getting down here."

"I didn't much feel like coming into work. How many have you sold exactly?"

I sold another just as she asked the question.

"Uh," I said, checking the notes I had made under the counter. "That was fifty-two."

"Fifty-two in three hours? Wow, we never used to sell fifty-two in a week. Still, at ten pence a copy, that's still only five pounds off my debt, Ro."

"A pound for a signed copy," I said. "Fifty-two pounds."

She blinked. "Fifty-two pounds in three hours?"

"Plus all the other stuff people keep buying. We're going to have to order in more rock, people seem to like it today."

"I ... I ... How? I mean, you have a poster and everything."

"I know, right? I had this idea last night and ran it past my dad. On the way in, I phoned Charm Pictures. I asked to speak with Mr Tyler, but it seems he's been suspended pending an enquiry. I spoke with Tina instead, you remember Tina?"

"Vaguely. Wasn't she Tyler's secretary?"

"Turns out she was the office supervisor or whatever they're called. Anyway, without Tyler, she's in charge. I made a deal with her, provisionally. I wanted to get you involved with the actual signing of any contracts. I ran the idea past her and she loved it, said she'd get a load of postcards sent, along with the poster."

"Ro, you're losing me. What deal?"

"Exclusive rights to these images. They have more than the one image, remember. Cara sold them a few. And I have the rest on a USB stick. They make the postcards, we make a fortune selling them. We can move into T-shirts, kites, towels, anything we can think of. Tina's almost as excited as I am about it all."

"No, no, no. Cara owns the copyright on the pictures."

"Cara doesn't have any photos left as proof. And if she owns up to taking them, she's going to be slapped with a lawsuit from Ms Yaren."

"What if Yaren pursues the lawsuit anyway?"

"She won't. I called her, too. I ran the idea past her and she couldn't stop laughing. She said her people had gone through all the pictures Cara had ever sold her and it turned out they'd only ever printed one set of photos before mine. They'd used that model from other photographers and called her up, found out it was legit. So if Yaren went after Cara, nothing much would happen. Cara doesn't have any money anyway. Yaren said this was a much better punishment, because Cara has absolutely no proof she ever took any photos in the first place."

"You've been busy. You've matured overnight."

"I know. You spent so long running around after me, I figured it was time I stood up and did something for myself."

"Do you think this will save the business?"

"You tell me. There are a lot of shops like ours on the Glazton seafront, Jas, but how many of them have their own set of exclusive racy postcards, endorsed by the sexy woman in the image? And yeah, I've finally decided to accept that I'm sexy, since everyone keeps telling me I am." I winked at her and this time knew I was doing it.

"Ro, this is insane."

"No, this is good business."

She inhaled deeply. "Can't argue with that."

"Jas, for the first time since all this began, I'm comfortable and I'm proud. And, as the poster says, this shop is the home of the Captain's Bombshell. This is where I belong."

"You may have to change the name of the shop, then."

"Me? What do you mean?"

"I meant what I said yesterday. I'm leaving for London. I was going to try to come to some kind of settlement with the bank, but if you carry on like this, you'll clear the debt and can continue working."

"No, you're staying with me. You have to."

"You don't need me."

"Jas," I said as she turned and walked slowly away. "Jas, no. Wait."

Sitting on the counter, I swung my legs over the side. There was a customer trying to buy something and I asked her to mind the shop. Without waiting for a reply, I ran after Jasmine. She was only a few steps away and she stopped.

"I'm not staying," she said without turning around.

"You have to. I'll accidentally burn down the shop by myself. I mean look, you only quit two seconds ago and I've already completely abandoned the till."

"Stop it," she said. "Stop trying to make this work. I'm not staying, Ro. I've tried to live here, at the seaside, and I've made a mess of everything."

"So running away is the answer? Was running away my answer when I had problems? I seem to recall I threw myself in the sea."

Jasmine took a deep breath and said nothing.

Knowing she would never turn to face me, I walked around to stand before her. She was still looking at the ground, so I gently raised her chin with my finger. "Jas, look at me. Please."

Her eyes were moist and I could see she really had come by the shop just to close up for good.

"Jas, I need you."

"No. You don't."

"And what about you? Don't you need me?"

"I ..." She closed her eyes while she tried to compose herself. When she opened them, she had not managed to at all. "I need you," she said in a small voice. "But I can't have you."

"Why not?"

"Please, Ro. If you haven't figured it out yet, I can't tell you. Look at you. You're achieving so much by yourself."

"So did you. You ran this shop for years, made a success of it until all the others opened. You achieved so much by yourself. Did it make you happy?"

"No."

"Then why would it make me happy?" When she did not answer, I said, "A wise woman once said I should cherish what I have. She said to make the most of every moment, do whatever makes me happiest and to promise her I'd never hide anything from the people I love." I paused. "Do you remember what I said to that?"

"I'm not the one with instant recall, Ro."

"I have sporadic instant recall. It happens whenever most convenient. What I replied, Jas, was that age doesn't matter much with love."

"Ro, I ..."

"Besides, I can't be in charge of anything, Jas. All I am is the Captain's Bombshell. It's the captain who's in charge."

Removing the white hat from my head, I turned it and placed it onto Jasmine's. She was a little shocked, but I did not allow her a moment to recover before I leant towards her. My lips touched hers gently and I tasted her tears and doubt. Placing one hand behind her head, the other upon the small of her back, I held her against me and melted into her body.

She pulled back and my hands fell away.

"Ro," she said, her eyes wide. "Ro, I ... What are ...?"

"Jasmine, please. Will you be my captain?"

She looked at me for some moments, emotions churning a maelstrom behind her eyes. Then she took a step towards me, placed her hand upon the back of my head and pressed her lips to mine. Our kiss was fierce, passionate, the culmination of years of sexual frustration for the both of us. Jasmine had loved me for a long time, I did not know how long, and somewhere deep in my heart I had always loved her. She was the one to whom I always turned when I was hurting. She was my rock, my best friend, my confidant. She was the woman who had saved me from suicide, who had given me a reason to go on living.

And in that instant, she also became my lover.

As we parted, my tongue lingered on her lower lip and I smiled. "You don't taste like chocolate, Jas. But there's always time."

"What's happened to you, Ro? You've changed."

"No. I've just stopped staring off into the sea whenever I have a problem. I've stopped daydreaming and opened my eyes to the joyful, wonderful, beautiful woman who makes my life complete."

I kissed her again and this time there was no doubt at all from either of us. We stood in that embrace for several long minutes, enjoying one another's company, the heat of the sun warming our bodies, the heat of our bodies warming each other. Above us, a seagull cawed, around us some of our customers were cheering.

"Sorry, Ro," someone called, "but we need some signatures over here."

Still holding firmly onto Jasmine as though to let her go would be to lose her forever, I turned my head to see my father was behind the counter. He was laying out some freshly baked cakes he had been busy making that morning and was handing them out for free to any customer who wanted one. There was something of a queue in the shop by this point, although none of the customers seemed to mind waiting.

"Ro?" he said. "Signatures?"

I wrinkled my nose, considered the matter, and said, "In a minute." Turning back to Jasmine, I found her grinning broadly. There were no more tears and I could feel her heart hammering against my breast. "Busy, Dad."

"I thought the shop was your way of building a future?"

"Yeah, but so's this."

"Wow," Jasmine said, "you really don't have *any* secrets from your father."

In answer, I leaned in for another kiss and closed my eyes. Life in Glazton was idyllic, life with my father was amazing, and life with Jasmine was perfection.

Only a few days earlier, I had tried to kill myself, but that was all in the past, just as Jasmine's assault was in the past, along with all the nonsense about that woman who had taken the photographs, whatever her had name had been.

Life was happiness, life was joy, life was bliss. In the arms of the most beautiful woman in the world, our bodies intertwined, our lips exploring our love, life was certainly worth living.

In Glazton, in one small shop along the seafront, two women had at last found love.

In the home of the Captain's Bombshell.

# AVAILABLE NOW IN PAPERBACK AND EBOOK

## Token Love

Best man on a stag party, Mark Fletcher has arranged a few days in the seaside town of Glazton. There amongst the flashing lights and empty promises he discovers Sandie Ford – a local young woman working at the prize counter of an amusement arcade. When Mark asks how many tokens he would need to exchange for her phone number, Sandie tells him ten thousand in an effort to get rid of him.

Mark, along with the stag Bill and their entire party, undertakes the mission to reach that goal.

Sandie's actions are applauded by her employer, Derek Reynard, who offers her a bonus if she leads Mark on, for every token earned is money spent. Feeling ashamed of her actions, Sandie attempts to find consolation in her colleague, Ruth; but Ruth – a stunning girl with her sights set on Vegas – does everything she can to support the venture, while at the same time trying her own luck with Mark.

As time runs out, Sandie faces the possibility that Mark might succeed in her challenge and agrees to meet with him so they can talk away from the gaudy deception of the arcades. Glazton may represent a holiday romance for Mark, but for Sandie it is a way of life; and a life perhaps she might be willing to change.

Everything depends on how determined Mark is to win the grand prize of Glazton.

## A Mermaid's Odyssey

Years ago, a heroic knight fell in love with a beautiful mermaid and a child was conceived.

Now, as her mother is murdered, eighteen-year-old Misako must flee her ocean home and venture into the land of the humans. Yet war has been raging between faeries and humans for generations and each side labels the hybrid girl a monster.

Emotionally unstable and without any guidance, she roams the land in search of her fabled father. Innocent and naïve, Misako quickly falls foul of human greed and immorality, while always striving to find the goodness in human hearts.

Her search takes her from fishermen to pirates, from mountains to forests. Every experience makes her stronger, every loss makes her weaker. She discovers the true horror of war and suffers the extreme hardships of being different. Ever searching for a place to belong, Misako refuses to give up hope of finding her father – the man who may not be quite the hero she needs.

A coming-of-age story about the love, fury and sadness of a child born of two races, but belonging to neither.

## Betty Stalks a Biker Cop

On her way home from work, Detective Jen Thompson rides her motorcycle between two brawling women. Taking one of them back to her flat overnight to recover, Thompson thinks she's doing a good deed; but Betty Carlington has other ideas. Distraught from breaking up with her girlfriend, Betty latches onto Thompson as her biker goddess and stalks her every move.

Enlisting the aid of her friend, Constable Sarah Brown, Detective Thompson tries everything she can to get Betty off her back. The more Thompson and Brown interact with Betty, the deeper they can see her problems lie. Feeling what she believes to be genuine love for Thompson, Betty's highly emotional state and naïve innocence threaten to destroy all their lives.

Torn between wanting to deter Betty's affections and not hurting her in the process, Thompson fights desperately to keep the situation a secret. Having suffered abuse all through her career for being a lesbian, Thompson is finally working in a department where her sexuality is never an issue. But if her colleagues find out a stalker has reduced her to a nervous wreck, her life could become unbearable.

With Thompson's life in Betty's hands, it's a race against time for the two bikers, where only one of them can cross the finish line intact.

## Sheriff Grizzly Ultimate Omnibus volume 1 of 3

His town: Grizzleton. His name: Bear. His secret: He's a grizzly bear wearing a sheriff's uniform ... but doesn't realise.

Collecting the first 4 Sheriff Grizzly stories. Join Bear, Deputy Rake and Doc Rum Tinkly as they protect Grizzleton (population 36) from outlaws, varmints and strange animal folk who turn up from time to time.

First, Bear and his posse must face the outlaw gang of Dirty Salvatore, who besets their town with a British invasion; a group of bally chums determined to bring the civility of cricket to the Wild West.

Then Bear has to deal with a bounty hunter who arrests Doc Tinkly's friend for horse theft. Tinkly and Deputy Rake (who'd do anything for her) sneak out to mount a rescue from neighbouring Townton: a lawless settlement with a penchant for hanging suspects without trial. Along the way, Tinkly suffers the effects of blue ice lollies, while Deputy Rake falls foul of the fictional folk hero Bandit-Man.

In book 3, Grizzleton's bank is robbed by the Coyote Colt Kid and one of Bear's deputies faces the blame. Only the Kid's former lover, Grizzleton's priest Father Yarek, can provide any hope to clear the deputy's name.

If you're still with us by this point, Deputy Rake and Doc Tinkly go to the circus while a mysterious lion-like stranger from Bear's past is determined to murder the poor sheriff.

All the while, Bear – a five-foot bundle of fur, fangs and feral fierceness – really can't understand why people seem to think he's a grizzly bear.

## One Week to Love: Speed Dating of the Gods

Living in the constant shadow of her younger, prettier sister, Rachael Cromwell is having terrible luck with men. Her life takes a strange turn when a sudden influx of attractive men are flung her way, only to be removed in mysterious circumstances. She has no idea that petulant higher beings have taken an interest in her pathetic love life, making a contest out of her misery.

Descending from Mount Olympus, the gods of Ancient Greece are playing with her emotions. Athena, goddess of wisdom and war, has one week to make Rachael fall in love with a detective named John Hatcher. Aphrodite, goddess of love, has one week to make sure that doesn't happen.

Meanwhile, Detective Hatcher is himself looking into a bizarre spate of murders involving Amazon soldiers working for both Athena and Aphrodite. His investigation leads him to the Cromwell sisters and together the three of them begin to unwind the truth concerning beings none of them even believe in.

Rachael Cromwell has never thought very highly of herself; she could never have imagined she would for one week become the object of a cross between a rom com and the Iliad.

## The Faerie Contract

Lisa Vale is an ordinary fifteen-year-old girl from a quiet rural village. She drinks at parties she shouldn't be at, has a tattoo her father doesn't know about and endures an annoying nine-year-old sister named Jenny.

When a strange girl named Aris protects her from a boy at a Christmas party, Lisa runs home in a panic. The following morning she discovers Aris has kidnapped Jenny in payment. To get her back, Lisa must convince Mayor Aldman to return the Christmas tree proudly displayed in the village square. For Aris is a hamadryad, a wood faerie whose very life is tied to the tree the mayor has invaded the faerie kingdom to acquire. Until Aris is returned home safely, she intends to keep Lisa's little sister in the faerie kingdom, slowly turning her into a creature of myth.

As Lisa investigates, she discovers the history of her village, and how the lineage of Aldmans and Vales stretches back many generations, to a terrible time when a deal was struck between man and faerie – a contract that neither can ever afford to break.

## Dinosaur World Omnibus

4 stories set on the quarantined dinosaur world of Ceres:

**Excavating a Dinosaur World:** Recently divorced and fighting a custody battle, Sara Garrel accepts an assignment to protect an archaeological expedition to the dinosaur world. Her charges are a stuffy professor, a spoiled rich gentleman and a flirtatious young student. But Garrel would put up with anything if it means earning enough money to win back her daughter.

**Dinosaur Fall-Girl:** When Professor Marigold Harper illegally enters Ceres in her search for the cure for cancer, a military unit is dispatched to bring her back. Separated from her unit, and with her escape shuttle wrecked by curious dinosaurs, Corporal Autumn is forced to drag the professor miles across hostile territory.

**Dinosaur Prison World:** Ashley Honeywood becomes the greatest dinosaur pit-fighter the Ceres penal colony has ever known. When her lover Garret Seward, the owner of the only decent eatery in the bayou, vanishes in a dinosaur attack, Honeywood heads out to find him.

**The Dinosaur That Wasn't:** A prison is seized by the inmates and Aubrey Whitsmith and Dexter Valentine find themselves in charge. When three soldiers arrive, they realise their dominancy might be about to collapse. But the soldiers are more interested with what's pursuing them through the swamp. For there is something out there, stalking them all.

## Have Imagination, Will Travel

Heather Tarne is not a witch – she just knows enough about the world around her to make sense of all the unexplainable things that happen in life.

This does not, however, stop Tarne and her friends from bouncing around realities, going from past, to future, to present and back around to the past in a series of bizarre stories which happily stop midway through and later pick up where they left off.

If that sounds confusing, imagine what it's like for Tarne. One moment she's negotiating peace treaties for a mediaeval king, the next she's playing a futuristic game of stick-in-the-mud with mutant snake people.

As the stories become stranger and stranger, Tarne begins to suspect this is not quite how life is meant to be. When a mysterious figure suggests there might be a reason for all her bouncing around between realities, Tarne looks to her group of friends and suspects one of them could be the cause of all her woes.

From spaceships to pirate ships, from detective agencies to super heroes, from Dark-Age brothels to reptile universities, Tarne's travels through reality are limited only by her imagination.

Ever trying to keep a level head, she's still (pretty) sure she's not a witch.

## Detective's Omnibus: 7 to Solve

Seven self-contained detective stories.

**Detective's Ex:** Lauren Corrigan's former lover, Detective Carl Robbins, refuses to look into the murder of a kind old man, so Lauren decides to solve the case herself.

**The Murder of Snowman Joe:** Cut off by an intense snowstorm, rural detective Felicity Hart calls in a retired big-city detective to catch a killer trapped in the village with them.

**Murder While You Wait:** A colleague is missing, so two detectives abandon their workload for what becomes their most bizarre investigation ever.

**One-Way Ticket to Murder:** Businessman. Teacher. Runaway. Ticket Inspector. One murder – four witnesses. All have a train to catch.

**The Murder of Loyalty:** Constable Caroline Lees lies to protect her boyfriend after a drunken brawl. When a body turns up, Lees fights to escape her own web of lies.

**The Woman Who Cried Diamonds:** Investigating a diamond theft, Detective Blake calls his ex-lover, former jewel thief Shenna Tarin; but soon suspects she may already be involved.

**Chasing the Shadow Man:** When an armed robbery goes wrong, a young girl is kidnapped and D.I. Jonathan Hope must team up with an old colleague if he's to get her back alive.

Printed in Great Britain
by Amazon